MARK KELLY

ASTRONAUT AND #1 *NEW YORK TIMES* BESTSELLING AUTHOR

READING
GUIDE I

PROJECT RESCUE

ASTROTWINS

ISBN 978-1-4814-2459-2

$7.99 U.S./$10.99 Can.

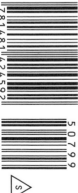

PRAISE FOR
ASTROTWINS—PROJECT RESCUE

"Readers will find themselves as invested in the kids' success as the team itself is. As before, infodumps on rocketry and politics fold themselves remarkably seamlessly into the narrative. From blastoff to landing, another nifty ride."　　*—Kirkus Reviews*

"Combining the knuckleheaded banter of the twins (based on Kelly and his brother) with adventure, camaraderie, and a firsthand knowledge of NASA technology, this chapter book offers space fans quite a ride."　　*—Booklist*

PRAISE FOR
ASTROTWINS—PROJECT BLASTOFF

"The information imparted is staged just right. Intriguing subject matter and rock-solid pacing combine for a nifty adventure—one that may well spark a new generation of astronauts."
—Kirkus Reviews

"From bickering twins to space-race history to a secret rocket-fuel formula, this chapter book offers an entertaining mixture of reality, historical fiction, science, and fun."　　*—Booklist*

"The characters are likable, the dialogue is enlightening as well as snappy, and the adventure is grand; a fine purchase for middle grade collections."　　*—School Library Journal*

"Realistic sibling and peer relationships, illuminating science, and some streamlined aeronautical history keep the story grounded—in a good way."　　*—Publishers Weekly*

MARK KELLY

WITH MARTHA FREEMAN

ASTROTWINS

PROJECT RESCUE

A PAULA WISEMAN BOOK
SIMON & SCHUSTER BOOKS
FOR YOUNG READERS

NEW YORK   LONDON   TORONTO
SYDNEY   NEW DELHI

SIMON & SCHUSTER BOOKS FOR YOUNG READERS
An imprint of Simon & Schuster Children's Publishing Division
1230 Avenue of the Americas, New York, New York 10020
This book is a work of fiction. Any references to historical events, real people, or real places are used fictitiously. Other names, characters, places, and events are products of the author's imagination, and any resemblance to actual events or places or persons, living or dead, is entirely coincidental.
Text copyright © 2016 by Mark Kelly
Cover illustration copyright © 2016 by Fernando Juarez
SIMON & SCHUSTER BOOKS FOR YOUNG READERS
is a trademark of Simon & Schuster, Inc.
For information about special discounts for bulk purchases, please contact Simon & Schuster Special Sales at 1-866-506-1949 or business@simonandschuster.com.
The Simon & Schuster Speakers Bureau can bring authors to your live event.
For more information or to book an event, contact the Simon & Schuster Speakers Bureau at 1-866-248-3049 or visit our website at www.simonspeakers.com.
Also available in a Simon & Schuster Books for Young Readers hardcover edition
Book design by Tom Daly
The text for this book was set in Minister Std.
Manufactured in the United States of America
0217 OFF
First Simon & Schuster Books for Young Readers paperback edition March 2017
2 4 6 8 10 9 7 5 3 1
The Library of Congress has cataloged the hardcover edition as follows:
Kelly, Mark E.
Astrotwins : project rescue / Mark Kelly with Martha Freeman.
pages cm.—(Astrotwins)
"A Paula Wiseman Book."
Includes bibliographical references.
Summary: "Mark Kelly and his twin brother are back for more outer space adventure, this time fixing up an abandoned Apollo command module and taking off to rescue a Russian cosmonaut who is stranded in space"—Provided by publisher.
ISBN 978-1-4814-2458-5 (hc)
1. Kelly, Mark E.—Childhood and youth—Juvenile fiction. 2. Kelly, Scott, 1964– —Childhood and youth—Juvenile fiction. [1. Kelly, Mark E.—Childhood and youth—Fiction. 2. Kelly, Scott, 1964– —Childhood and youth—Fiction. 3. Brothers—Fiction. 4. Twins—Fiction. 5. Space flight—Fiction. 6. Rockets (Aeronautics)—Fiction. 7. Grandfathers—Fiction.] I. Freeman, Martha, 1956– II. Title. III. Title: Project rescue.
PZ7.K296395Asw 2016
[Fic]—dc23
2015017968
ISBN 978-1-4814-2459-2 (pbk)
ISBN 978-1-4814-2460-8 (eBook)

Dedicated to all of the math and science teachers out there!
Your work is so important to the success of our nation.
—M. K.

CHAPTER 1

SATURDAY, MARCH 28, 1976

Mark Kelly was doing his best to save his dog's life, but his dog—a big brown mutt named Major Nelson—did not want to be saved. Again and again, Mark fastened the clear plastic oxygen mask over his nose. Again and again, Major Nelson shook it off.

"Can I get some help here?" Mark asked his twin brother, Scott.

It was after lunch, and the two twelve-year-olds were kneeling on the carpet in the living room of their house. Sprawled between them, Major Nelson thumped his tail; dog rescue was the best game yet!

"If I help, it'll spoil my entertainment," Scott said. "You're better than watching *Happy Days* on TV."

The boys had a real oxygen mask, one with perforations to allow air flow. But in place of an oxygen tank, they were using a big soda bottle, its cap replaced by a valve made out of cardboard discs. For tubing, they had taped together plastic drinking straws. The flimsy homemade setup didn't look very realistic, but it gave the boys a way to practice for tests in their Red Cross first-aid class—or, for that matter, real emergencies.

"You are not very funny," Mark told Scott. "Now do me a favor and keep the mask on his nose while I hook everything up."

Scott did as his brother directed while at the same time scratching Major Nelson behind the ears. "You're a good dog—yes, you are!"

"Woof," Major Nelson agreed.

"Ha!" Mark pumped his fist. "He's connected! How long did that take, do you think?"

Scott shook his head and sighed. "Too long. Our dog is dead."

"Oh, cut it out," Mark said. "Maybe when Mom gets home she'll let us practice on her."

"You know she'll say she's too busy," Scott said. "And besides, we don't have that much time. We gotta meet Barry at the library at two thirty."

Mark made a face. "I forgot about that. Can you believe we have to go to the library? *Again?*"

"I know. I thought we were done with libraries forever after all the research we did last summer. But if we're going to write that report, we need to," Scott said.

Mark's face brightened. "I just thought of something. Barry's a brainiac! He can do all the hard parts, and we'll just draw pictures or something."

"You? Draw pictures?" Scott said.

"Yeah, okay, *you* draw the pictures," Mark said. "And I'll, uh . . . write my name on the top. How does that sound?"

"You probably can't screw up writing your name," said Scott, "even if you did suffocate Major Nelson."

"Don't blame me. The mask was made for a human, not a canine," Mark said.

"We could practice on each other," Scott said, "and since it's my turn, you're the one who has to lie down, be quiet, and pretend you're super sick. Ready—go!"

Mark shook his head. "Like I'm gonna let you press that thing on my face! Why would I even trust you?"

"Uh . . . because I'm the only brother you've got? And I trusted you when I went into space last fall."

"At least you had a clean faceplate on your helmet," said Mark. "This mask is gross—covered with dog drool."

"Woof," said Major Nelson.

"Aw, look, you've hurt his feelings." Scott waved the mask as if he was about to clamp it over his brother's nose, his brother swerved out of the way, Scott hooked him by the elbow, Mark lunged, and an instant later the two boys were on the floor, wrestling . . . much to the delight of Major Nelson, who howled his encouragement.

The match, punctuated by thumps, bumps, and grunts, came to an abrupt end when Mom appeared in the doorway. "Boys?"

Mark was out of breath but still managed to say, "He started it!"

Scott, also breathless, objected: "That's not true!"

"Oh yeah?" Mark said. "You can ask Major Nelson, Mom. He saw the whole thing."

"Well, maybe I did start it," Scott admitted, "but I'm not the one with a bad attitude about first-aid class."

"At least I practice," Mark said. "You just sit back and watch."

"Yeah—watch you suffocate patients," Scott said. "I just hope to heck you never have to save anybody for real, 'cause if you do, they're done for."

"Hold on a second." Mom had been eyeing her sons from the doorway. Now she came into the room and sat down on the sofa. "I thought you guys liked the class."

"We do," Scott said quickly.

"Said the kiss-up," said Mark.

"I am not a kiss-up," said Scott.

"Yeah, you are," said Mark.

Mom raised her hand. "Leaving that aside for now—what gives with the class?"

"It's just we're never gonna have to use this stuff," Mark said.

Scott chimed in. "Nobody counts on kids to save lives,

Mom. They count on doctors and nurses and ambulance people. They count on cops sometimes. But we're not old enough for those jobs."

Mom cocked her head and smiled. "This line of reasoning's kind of funny coming from you two."

Mark by this time had sat up and assessed his injuries. There seemed to be a bruise on his shoulder and another on his head, but that was okay. He was pretty sure he had given as good as he got. "What do you mean?" he asked his mom.

"I think she means the whole space thing," Scott said. "I think she means Project Blastoff was a grown-up thing to do."

Mom nodded. "That's exactly what I mean. Going into space is something not many kids have done."

"Technically, it's something *no* kids have done . . . except Scott," Mark said.

"I rest my case," said Mom.

Sometimes each twin could tell what the other was thinking. Now they looked at each other and decided without a word that Scott should ask their mom the obvious question: "Uh, what's your point?"

"That you boys get yourselves into more than the usual number of tough situations," Mom said, "and I know from experience what a lousy feeling it is when somebody needs help and you don't know what to do. This class is going to give you the knowledge you need to be helpful. And I bet one day, sooner or later, that knowledge is going to come in handy."

Scott Kelly never mentioned it to anyone, but he had a mental filing system for grown-ups' comments. That little speech of his mom's he filed in the category: Stuff I Probably Should've Paid Attention To.

And the way things turned out, he was absolutely right.

CHAPTER 2

The Kelly family lived in West Orange, New Jersey. On the map, it wasn't far from the lights, grit, and action of New York City, but on the ground it seemed to be a world away. The Kellys' street was quiet and tree-lined. On it were a few dozen modest two-story houses, all of them built in the 1940s and 1950s. Most of the neighbors had dogs and kids, a car or two in the garage, and well-kept yards, front and back. The Kelly house was gray stone with white wood trim.

Scott and Mark's parents were both police officers who worked long hours. Two years before, when their mom got her job, she became the first female police officer on the local force. Mark and Scott had no siblings. According to their parents, two kids were plenty when the two happened to be as energetic and independent as the twins.

Up till the previous summer, the twins were mostly known for getting in trouble. Then one day in July their grandpa Joe, their mom's father, had suggested they might fight less if they worked together on some big project. How about if they built a go-kart?

The go-kart idea was not very inspiring.

But the twins had been interested in space exploration ever since they were little and watched Neil Armstrong and Buzz Aldrin on the moon.

"Fine," Grandpa Joe had said. "Build a spaceship, then. You can use my barn."

Then he'd gone back to reading his newspaper.

Before they entirely understood what they were getting into, Mark and Scott were devoting every minute and every ounce of skill and brainpower they possessed to an insane goal: building a spacecraft to launch into orbit.

They named their plan Project Blastoff and the spaceship *Crazy 8*. The whole thing was crazy, after all, and eight people had done most of the work. Besides the boys, they included Jenny, a girl the twins had nicknamed Egg, who was determined for once to win her school science fair; two friends of hers, Howard and Lisa; Lisa's dad, who owned an auto repair shop; their own brainiac friend, Barry; and Barry's Vietnam vet brother, Tommy.

Project Blastoff did not exactly go smoothly. There were times they wanted to quit. There were disagreements and scary moments. There were tons of surprises. But in the end, they were successful—so successful that Jenny's mom, Mrs. O'Malley, told them someday they might be asked to help out with a U.S. government space project.

"Till then, you have to stay prepared," she told them. "That means plenty of exercise, good food, keeping up with your studies—especially math and science. Oh— and pay attention to the news, too, especially anything to do with the space program."

Thinking about it now, Scott thought Mrs. O'Malley had sounded a lot like Mom when she talked about the first-aid class. Grown-ups were forever telling him and Mark to be ready for stuff that didn't happen.

By now it had been five months since *Crazy 8* had orbited. At first, Scott and Mark had awoken every morning wondering if this was the day they'd get a phone call from NASA, the U.S. government space agency. But the call didn't come, and lately they had stopped waking up hopeful. In fact, they were feeling discouraged. Mark and Scott Kelly had turned twelve in February. Was it possible the most exciting adventure of their lives was already behind them?

"If you're going to the main library on Mt. Pleasant Avenue, I can drop you off," Mom offered. "The calendar says almost spring, but it sure is cold out."

"We can ride bikes," Mark said.

"Are your lights working?" Mom asked. "Reflectors in place? You might end up riding back at dusk."

"Of course, Mom! Aren't we always super careful?" Mark asked.

Mom's answer was to raise her eyebrows.

"Don't worry," Scott said. "It's like you said about that class. With our new skills, we are prepared to fix any injuries we get. I mean, didn't Mark just kill Major Nelson and bring him back from the dead?"

Mom was right about the cold, but the boys believed jackets were for sissies and almost never wore them. To keep warm, they pedaled extra hard. This made the ride a quick one, but even so, their friend Barry was seated at a table taking notes when they walked into the main reading room.

"Are we late?" Mark took the chair beside Barry, and Scott sat down across the table.

"Nah. I was early. I wanted to get out of the house. Tommy and my mom . . ." Barry shrugged.

"Are they arguing again?" Scott asked. "I thought everybody was getting along better after he helped us with *Crazy 8*." Tommy, who had served in the air force, had provided flying tips and helped them figure out who would make the best astronaut.

"It was better for a while, but now Mom and Dad say

Tommy needs to get a job," Barry said, "and Tommy just can't seem to get motivated."

Scott said, "I'm sorry. That's rough."

Mark shifted in his seat, then nodded at the magazine on the table. "What are you reading?"

Barry flipped over the magazine to reveal the cover. It was a five-year-old copy of *TIME*. The photo showed the three Russian cosmonauts who had flown a mission called *Soyuz 11* that year, 1971. The report the three boys were working on was about the Soviet and American space programs, and they had already done some research in the school library.

"Those guys are the ones who died, right?" Scott said.

Barry nodded. "Something went wrong, and two bolts fired at the same time. All that force blew open a valve, and their oxygen leaked out." He shrugged. "You can't live without oxygen."

Hearing this, Scott felt his heart bump. Only a few people in the whole world had felt the thrust of a rocket pushing them into orbit, seen the cloud-covered sapphire blue oceans from above, and floated in zero gravity. Scott was one of them. So were those three men. And even though they were from a faraway country—a country many Americans thought of as an enemy—he felt the connection.

Mark looked from Barry's serious face to Scott's. "Guys?" he said. "So far coming to the library has been a total bummer. Can we maybe think about something more fun?"

"Here's a fun idea," said Barry. "How about if we write a research report?"

"You have a weird idea of fun," said Mark.

"Is that news to you?" said Barry.

"Anyway, it will make Mr. Hackess happy," said Scott. Mr. Hackess was the boys' sixth-grade teacher.

"Scott and I planned the whole thing out before we got here," said Mark. "First off, I'm in charge because I have proven leadership potential. Second, Barry does the actual researching and writing because, let's face it, he's the smart one. Third, Scott will draw the pictures."

"Can you draw?" Barry looked at Scott.

Scott shook his head no. "This is all my brother's idea."

"Have you guys got wax in your ears or something?" Mark asked. "What I said was: lead-er-ship po-ten-tial."

"Unh-hunh," said Barry. "How about we try it my way instead? Scott finds the old newspapers we need on microfilm, and Mark gets new information from the files of current newspapers. We need to be up to date on Salyut, the Soviet mission that's in orbit now. After that, you both write your notes, and then we can get together to outline the report, maybe even write a rough draft."

"Wait a sec," Mark said. "How long are we gonna be stuck at the library, anyway? The paper's not even due till Wednesday."

"If you guys get off your rear ends," Barry said, "we'll be home in time for dinner."

In spite of Mark's grumbling, Barry turned out to be right. By five thirty, when the library closed, the boys had completed a draft, and Scott, who had the best handwriting, had agreed he'd recopy it.

This is the report turned in by Barry Leibovitz, and Mark and Scott Kelly, the following Wednesday morning:

The Soviet Union, also known as Russia or the U.S.S.R., has a space program. So does the United States, also known as America. In the Soviet Union, astronauts are called cosmonauts.

No Russian has ever gone to the moon. But the Russians have still done a good job with their program. Here are some examples. A Soviet satellite named Sputnik was the first satellite in space. A Soviet dog named Laika was the first dog in space. A Soviet cosmonaut named Yuri Gargarin was the first person in space. Yuri Gargarin's spaceship, Vostok 1, went up and came down after one orbit in 1961.

American spacecraft land in the water. Russian ones land on land. You need to understand this because something funny happened when Mr. Gargarin landed. He was off course and floated down by parachute in the countryside. Two women saw him float down. He was wearing an orange flight suit and a big helmet. He looked scary like an alien. He didn't want the women to run away, so he said, "I am a Soviet citizen like you, who has descended from space, and I must find a telephone to call Moscow!"

The two women helped him find a telephone.

Today, the United States and the Soviet Union both have space stations. The American one is called Skylab. It was launched three years ago, in 1973. Skylab is still up in orbit today, but currently no one is home.

So far, three missions have visited Skylab. The astronauts who stayed in it the longest stayed for twelve weeks. They even spent Christmas there. They did many science experiments. They enjoyed looking out the window. They rode an exercise bicycle to keep their muscles strong.

The Russian space station program is called Salyut. "Salyut" means "fireworks" in the Russian language. There is only one Skylab, but there have been four Salyut space stations so far, and there might be more, only we don't know for sure because the Russians don't always tell the rest of the world what is going on.

The first Salyut space station launched in 1971, two years before Skylab. So when it comes to space stations, the Russians were first (again). However, many things have gone wrong in the Salyut program. For example, one time Russian cosmonauts flew all the way to the space station and couldn't get their spacecraft to connect up with it, so they had to turn around and fly all the way home.

The most recent Salyut went into orbit in December 1974. It is still up there like Skylab (only in a different place). Two crews of cosmonauts have visited it and gone home. Now a cosmonaut named Ilya Ilyushin is there.

Basically, the American Skylab and the Russian Salyut have the same main purpose. They are supposed to help scientists figure out how people can be healthy in space for a long time. If people are ever going to go on long space journeys like they show on TV shows, this will be necessary. The other purpose is for science experiments and observation. For example, it is easier to observe the sun from space where there is no air to blur the view.

It used to be that the Russian and the American space programs competed with each other. This was called the space race. However, last summer a Russian Soyuz met up with an American Apollo spacecraft in space, and the astronauts and cosmonauts inside shook hands and ate together, so now we are all friends. At least for now . . . and at least while we are in space.

CHAPTER 3

FRIDAY, APRIL 2, 1976

As usual on a school morning, Scott and Mark came in for breakfast a few minutes before eight o'clock. They were dressed but rumpled. It was unclear whether they had combed their hair.

Mom had worked the night shift the previous day. Early in the morning she awakened the twins, said hello–good-bye to them, and went off to bed to catch a few hours of sleep.

This left Dad in charge of breakfast. Now he set out cereal bowls, milk, and orange juice on the table in the kitchen. The boys sat down and poured cereal, Cap'n Crunch for Mark, Frosted Flakes for Scott.

"Hey, pass me the milk, okay?" Scott asked his brother.

Standing by the sink, Mr. Kelly rubbed his ears.

"Funny. I didn't hear my own son say 'please.'"

Scott rolled his eyes. *"Please."*

"Sarcastic people don't get milk, do they?" Mark appealed to his dad.

"Sheesh, I'll grab it myself," Scott said, and he reached across Mark, who batted his arm away, causing Scott to tip over sideways. To steady himself, he slapped his hand on the table . . . and knocked the milk carton to the floor.

Milk splashed everywhere, and both boys spoke at once: "It's his fault!"

Mr. Kelly sighed. "I'd have to say you're both right there. And you'll both be cleaning up, too. *Pronto*—or you won't have time for breakfast at all."

The twins made enough messes that they had cleanup down to a system. Scott grabbed a sponge. Mark got the paper towels.

Meanwhile, Major Nelson, who had been dozing in the corner by the back door, lifted his head and laid it down again. Spilled milk did not deserve further investigation.

"You know, you knuckleheads have been at each other a lot lately," Mr. Kelly said to his sons. "Is everything okay?"

"Sure, fine." Mark threw the sodden mass of paper towels into the wastebasket under the kitchen sink.

"There's just nothing much exciting going on." Scott sat down again and grabbed the box of Frosted Flakes.

"When does baseball season start?" Dad asked.

"Tryouts are next week," said Mark. "But Scott will never make the team. He's turned into a big klutz."

Scott looked up. "Take that back."

"Who tripped over his own sneakers last night?" said Mark.

Scott rose partway out of his chair and brandished the cereal spoon. "I *said* take that—"

Dad raised his hand. "I am going to turn on the news," he said, "and you two are going to observe absolute and total silence. Got it?"

On a shelf above the kitchen counter was a portable TV. Dad reached up and switched it on. There was a pause while the tube warmed up, then *Today* show host Barbara Walters appeared in twelve-inch black-and-white glory.

Even though the boys weren't especially interested in news, they couldn't help glancing at the screen. Then, when they grasped what Barbara Walters was saying, they both stopped eating.

". . . known about Ilya Ilyushin, a cosmonaut thought to be trapped inside the Salyut space station now orbiting some 220 miles above the surface of Earth. NASA says it has no information on the purpose of Ilyushin's mission. A spokesman would confirm only that the cosmonaut's Soyuz spacecraft launched from the Baikonur Cosmodrome in the Kazakhstan republic of the Soviet Union two weeks ago.

"Now to NBC's Jay Barbree at the Kennedy Space Center. Good morning, Jay. What is NASA telling us about what went wrong with the Soviet mission?"

"Good morning, Barbara. To answer your question, NASA isn't telling us much at all. Whether that's because the Soviet authorities aren't sharing information or for some other reason, we're not sure.

"Earlier, I talked to a noted space expert who reminded me that spacecraft are such complex pieces of machinery, any number of problems might have arisen. Perhaps there has been a meteorite strike. Perhaps a piece of equipment shook loose during launch. Perhaps one of the experiments on board has caused an electrical short circuit—"

Barbara cut in. "Did you say 'experiments,' Jay?"

"I did say 'experiments,' Barbara."

"Any word as to the nature of those experiments?"

"That's a negative, Barbara. Indeed, this has been a very frustrating story to report. Soviet authorities are not accustomed to Western-style press freedoms. If the experiments are like those aboard previous Salyut stations, it's likely they are biological in nature. Like their counterparts in the United States, the Russians are interested in how spaceflight and zero gravity affect various organisms and organic systems.

"At the same time, there are other possibilities. . . ."

"What would those be, Jay?" Barbara asked.

"Well, some in U.S. government circles have speculated that the Soviet space program has a secret military purpose. If that's so, it opens the door to all sorts of experimental possibilities, from espionage to weaponry."

"Scary stuff, Jay," said Barbara.

"There is that potential," said Jay.

"And are there plans for a rescue mission? Should rescue become necessary, that is," said Barbara.

"None have been released at this time," Jay said. "Now, back to you, Barbara."

"Thanks, Jay." Barbara appeared on the screen again. "Repeating this hour's top story, an unspecified mechanical problem on the Russian Salyut space station reportedly has marooned the lone cosmonaut inside, leaving him as of now with no means of returning to Earth.

"Russian authorities say they are confident the problem can be fixed, and in the meantime, Cosmonaut Ilya Ilyushin remains in good health and good spirits. I'm sure I speak for all Americans when I say we're holding a good thought for the stranded space traveler.

"In other news—"

CHAPTER 4

The boys never learned what the other news was. They had stopped listening. Mark was imagining himself suited up and spacewalking to the rescue of Ilya Ilyushin. Scott was feeling bad for a guy who was all by himself looking through Salyut's window at Earth, wondering if he'd ever see his home again.

It was eight twenty by this time, and school started at eight forty-five. Dad looked over his shoulder to ask whether the Salyut mission was the one the boys and Barry had written their report on. But before he could finish the question, he noticed Scott's and Mark's cereal bowls were practically full. "What is with you knuckleheads? At this rate, you're gonna miss the bus!"

"Do you think NASA has a rocket ready on the pad

that could maybe rescue that cosmonaut?" Mark asked, and at the same time Scott said, "Do you know if Ilya Ilyushin has kids?"

"Your sympathy for that Russian is admirable," Dad said, "but he'll still be stuck after school. Now slurp up, grab your lunches, and get moving!"

The math lesson that morning was ratios. "If the ratio of girls to boys in the class is three to two, and there are nine girls, how many boys are there?"

"Not enough," Mark answered, causing most of the boys to laugh and most of the girls to roll their eyes.

"Very funny, Mark Kelly," said Mr. Hackess. "Do you want to try expressing that in numerical form?"

"He means do the problem," said Barry helpfully.

Mark thought for a second. "Six boys."

"Genius in our midst," said Scott, under his breath.

"What was that, Scott?" Mr. Hackess raised his eyebrows.

"My brother is a genius," Scott said.

"You take that back," Mark said.

Mary Anne, a dark-haired girl with brown eyes who sat in the front row, swiveled around to look at Mark. "I think 'genius' is usually a compliment."

"I would think so too, except my brother's being sarcastic," Mark said.

"No, I wasn't. You got the problem right," Scott said, "for once."

"Everyone in the class got the problem right, didn't they?" said Barry. "It's easy."

"Moving on . . . ," said Mr. Hackess.

The boys had done their homework, most of it anyway, and Mr. Hackess was doing a decent job at the blackboard, too. Even so, after a few minutes, both Mark and Scott's minds began to wander and they looked out the window.

Last summer when they had had to do math to build and fly *Crazy 8*, they had picked it up quickly. But now the best rewards they could hope for were an A on a test and a "Good going!" from Mom and Dad.

Getting As on tests was nice, and Mom and Dad were nice too. But as incentives, they just couldn't compete with space travel, and sometimes—like today—the boys had a hard time paying attention in class.

At lunchtime, it was raining outside, so the whole school had to squeeze into the cafeteria and eat together, no recess. The room was damp, hot, and sticky. The fluorescent lighting turned everybody's carrots, chips, and sandwiches a sick shade of pale green.

"When's Hackess handing back our reports, anyway?" Barry swung his leg over the metal bench across the table from Mark. Scott had taken a seat at the other end of the same table.

"Beats me," Mark said. "Did you hear on the news about that Ilya cosmonaut guy?"

Barry bit into his sandwich. "We should rescue him, whaddaya think?" he said with his mouth full.

"'We' you and me, or 'we' the United States of America?" Mark asked. "And would you mind closing your mouth, please?"

Barry deliberately opened wide to display a whole lot of half-chewed tuna salad.

Mark cringed. *"Gross!"*

Barry laughed, swallowed, and wiped his mouth with his napkin. "'We' meaning you and me and Egg and Scott and everybody. It would be a good project for Tommy, too—get him out of his funk. That's what my mom calls it."

"One problem." Scott had been listening in. "We don't happen to have a spacecraft anymore."

"What happened to it?" a fifth grader named Karen asked. The *Crazy 8* mission had made national news in the fall, and for a while Barry and the twins had been major school celebrities.

"The government came with a helicopter and fished it out of Greenwood Lake. That's by where our grandpa lives, the lake where Scott splashed down," Mark explained. "After that, I don't really know."

"NASA's probably studying it for tips on engineering," Barry said.

"Wherever it is, it's too beat-up and burnt-up to fly

again," said Mark. "We built it to be like a Mercury spacecraft, a one-shot deal."

"Maybe NASA would lend us a shiny new spacecraft," Scott said, "if they've got a spare lying around."

"You wouldn't want to go up in space again, would you, Scott?" said another fifth grader at the table, Michael. "It's pretty dangerous, right?"

Scott didn't hesitate. "Yeah, I want to go again! It's the best thing I ever did."

"Hey," said Barry, "what about if this time the brainiac gets his turn?"

Mark jumped in, "Unh-unh, this time *I'm* up! With *Crazy 8*, I got robbed."

"Uh, guys?" Scott said. "Just to remind you, as far as anybody knows, there is no 'this time.'"

"Besides," said the boy named Michael, "that Ilya guy's not even an American. My mom says Russians are communists, and you can't trust 'em. She says the Russians ought to rescue their own cosmonaut."

Some of the kids at the table nodded, but Scott frowned and Mark suddenly noticed how uncomfortably his tailbone was pressed against the narrow metal bench.

Quietly, Barry said, "Communist or not, he's a person, and he's in a lot of trouble."

CHAPTER 5

When Scott thought back on it later, he decided Project Rescue really started with that kid Michael's comment at lunch. As Grandpa Joe would have said, it stuck in his craw. And all that afternoon—whether he was labeling a volcano on a map or calculating more ratios—he was actually thinking about what Barry had said, and he was thinking that Barry was right.

What mattered about people was that they were people—not what country they were born in or what politics they liked. That seemed especially obvious when you pictured someone stranded all alone in cold, unforgiving space.

Mark, on the other hand, wasn't thinking about Michael's comment, or Barry's, either. His thoughts were all over the place. Would he make the baseball team that year? Would there be corned beef and cabbage again for dinner? Would the weather clear up enough for bike riding after school?

Mark even wondered when Hackess would give back the reports and what grade they were going to get. Not that he would ever admit to Barry or Scott that he cared about that kind of stuff.

But despite his scattered thoughts, Mark understood right away when he and his brother got home from school and his brother said, "We could call Mrs. O'Malley."

Peggy O'Malley was the mother of Jenny, nicknamed Egg because she was an egghead. Egg had been the third member of the *Crazy 8* team—right after the twins themselves. It was Egg's mom who turned out to have the government connections that had kept them from getting in trouble for launching an unauthorized spaceship. It was Egg's mom who had said NASA might want their help on future missions.

Along with Howard and Lisa, the O'Malleys lived in West Milford, New Jersey, near the *Crazy 8* launch site at Greenwood Lake. By car, it was about ninety minutes away from the Kellys' house, and what with school and their parents' jobs, the twins hadn't been up there since November.

"Would calling Mrs. O'Malley do any good, do you think?" Mark asked Scott.

The boys were sitting at the kitchen table again. Both their parents were out—their dad at work and their mom, according to the note on the fridge, running errands and back soon. They were drinking milk and eating apples. The rule was they each had to eat a whole apple before they could get out the Oreos.

"Maybe Mrs. O'Malley will know more about what's going on than they had on the news," Scott said.

Mark smiled. "You can't pull that on me, Scott Kelly. I'm your brother, remember? What you're really saying is let's remind Mrs. O'Malley we're available to fly to the rescue . . . just in case NASA's forgotten all about us."

Scott returned the grin. "It can't hurt to ask."

"Nah, it can't, *except* that Mom and Dad'll never let us phone her," Mark said. "It's long-distance, remember? Too expensive, they'll say."

The boys were discussing how to get around the long-distance problem when, arms full of groceries, Mom shouldered the back door open.

Scott was on his feet in an instant. "Is there more to bring in? Can I help?"

Mom set the bags on the kitchen counter, then turned toward her sons. "Out with it, Scott. Either you've done something or you want something."

"He wants the helpful-twin-of-the-year award," Mark put in. "I'd try for it too, but I'm not a big enough kiss-up to compete."

"If offering to help is kissing up, I'm all in favor," Mom said. "But this is all the groceries, so you're off the hook."

"Okay, well, in that case . . . ," Scott spoke quickly. "Can we call Jenny's mom? Mrs. O'Malley, I mean? I know it's long-distance, but I have some birthday money left, and Mark says he'll clean the bathroom for a month to pay back his share."

Mark said, "Hang on about that bathroom part—"

But Mom was already nodding. "When I heard the news about that cosmonaut, I thought you might want to phone Egg's mom. It's okay with me. Go ahead."

Mark and Scott looked at each other. Was their mom feeling okay? "What about how long-distance phone calls cost money?" Mark asked.

"This is an emergency," Mom said. "There might be something you can do to help—something short of going to the rescue, I hope. That sounds dangerous."

Mark and Scott didn't hesitate. They were afraid Mom would change her mind.

"You get on the extension!" Mark told his brother, who headed down the hall to his parents' room without any argument.

Mom's address book was in a kitchen drawer. Mark pulled it out, found the O'Malleys' number, dialed, and listened to the rings: One . . . two . . . three . . .

Maybe Mrs. O'Malley was away on a business trip.

Was Mrs. O'Malley some kind of big shot? Mark had always wondered. . . .

It wasn't till the fifth ring that a familiar voice answered. "Hello?"

"Egg, hi, it's Mark—Mark Kelly!"

"Scott Kelly too," his brother chimed in.

"Oh, you guys!" Egg said. "It's so great to hear from you. Is everything okay? Are you calling about the cosmonaut? 'Cause if you are—guess what—I've got news, news and a big surprise."

CHAPTER 6

The next day was Saturday. Since for once Mr. and Mrs. Kelly both had the day off, it was all four Kellys who piled into the family's Ford Country Squire station wagon at seven a.m., picked Barry up at his house a few blocks away, and headed west on Highway 80, then north on 287 toward Grandpa Joe's house at Greenwood Lake.

All three boys were excited about the day trip—excited enough that they hadn't even minded getting up super early on a weekend.

"Tell me again what Egg told you on the phone yesterday," Barry said. He was squeezed between the twins in the backseat. "Her exact words this time."

"I'm not sure I can remember her exact words," Mark said.

"Me neither," said Scott. "I think I was kind of in shock

after our conversation, like my brain got scrambled."

"For your brain, that's not shock, that's normal," Mark said.

Scott ignored his brother. "Egg said something like how she and Howard and Lisa had a surprise for us, and because of the whole cosmonaut thing they were going to tell us earlier than they planned to."

"I think Egg said they got help from her mom even," Mark said. "The only exact word I remember her using is 'big.' I'm sure she said that: 'big.'"

"You know," Mom said, "I hear from my dad—your grandpa Joe—pretty often. He's mentioned the O'Malleys more than once, but never anything about a big surprise. Of course, my father is pretty good at keeping his mouth shut."

"Can we turn on the radio, Dad?" Scott asked. "Maybe there's more news from space."

"Yeah, it could be by now the Soviets have made the repairs themselves," Barry said.

"Hope not," Mark said.

"Seriously?" Barry looked at Mark.

"Don't get me wrong. I want the guy to be okay," Mark said. "It's just—"

"—just that you want the chance to play hero." Scott finished his sentence.

"That's not it at all," Mark said.

"Yeah, it is," Scott said.

"No, it isn't," Mark said.

"*Ow!*" said Barry.

"Sorry," said Scott. "I meant to kick my brother."

"Boys?" Mom looked over her shoulder—a warning look. The twins shot her their most innocent smiles, and she turned her attention to the radio. First she found an old Elton John song, "Rocket Man," which seemed appropriate. After that there was the weather forecast, clearing with highs in the forties. When finally the news came on, the cosmonaut got only brief mention. Still up there. Still stuck. Mechanical problem still unknown.

The only new piece of information was this: "Russian sources refuse to comment, but a noted American space expert says the Salyut station typically can provide breathable air for about thirty days.

"Provided first that the spacecraft has not sprung a leak and second that the cosmonaut does not overexert himself, he should be able to survive comfortably for approximately eleven more."

All three boys had the same thought: eleven more days, and after that . . . what?

It was a few minutes before nine o'clock, still early by the twins' weekend standards, when the Kelly family's station wagon turned off the road onto Grandpa's unpaved driveway. Dad had barely set the parking brake when

Scott and Mark tore off their seat belts and blasted out of confinement in the backseat.

Barry was not far behind.

For his part, Grandpa must have been watching, because only a moment later the front door flew open, and he rushed down the path to meet them.

A widower who lived by himself, Joe McAvoy had never been much on hugging . . . until the *Crazy 8* orbit in the fall. Mom said she had always wondered what it would take to touch the old coot's heart, and now she knew: It took one of his precious grandsons returning from space in a homemade rocket.

Grandpa Joe clasped the twins in a grizzly-size bear hug, then backed away to get a better look. "You've gone and done it again," he sighed. "Grown some more, I mean. You do it even though you know darned well that it makes an old man feel older."

"We can't help it, Grandpa," Mark said.

"We'd stop if we could," Scott added. "Who wants to be a boring old grown-up anyway?"

"Darned right. Better to stay a kid. Lord knows I'm doing my best." Grandpa straightened up and looked over the twins' heads. "And here you've brought your pal Barry, and he's grown too."

"It's good to see you, Mr. McAvoy," said Barry.

"Good to see you too, son, even if you are six inches taller than you were in the fall. Who else did you bring with you? Why—who'd've thunk, there're your parents! Where've you all been hiding yourselves, anyway? And don't say 'work.' Work is a pretty weak excuse."

"Easy for the retired guy to say, Joe." Dad slapped Grandpa on the back, and Mom gave him a quick kiss on his unshaved cheek.

Grandpa was indignant. "Retired? I'm busier than I've ever been in my life!" he said, and as they all walked up the path to the house, he recounted the projects he had going—everything from rototilling the garden patch to fixing up his classic truck.

Meanwhile, as the radio weather had predicted, the gray clouds broke to reveal patches of blue sky. They were almost to the front door when the sunshine caused something out beyond the fir trees to flash white.

"What's that?" Mark pointed. "Over toward the lake?"

Grandpa replied, "Nothing," then put his hand on the small of Mark's back and tried to nudge him toward the house.

Mark would not be nudged. "You didn't even look, Grandpa! See it, Barry? Over by the launch site—or near it, anyway."

By now Mom, Dad, and Scott were looking too. "Whatever it is must be awfully tall," Mom said.

Suddenly, Scott felt as if the air had been sucked from his chest. "Wait a sec. Grandpa, is that the surprise?"

"Nope." Grandpa had stopped walking but still

refused to look. "That is, what surprise? I don't know about any surprise."

Mom bit back a smile. "You may be good at keeping your mouth shut, Dad, but you are the world's worst liar." Her words were just out when everyone heard the sound of tires on gravel behind them. A car was coming up the driveway.

CHAPTER 7

"Phew, that is a beauty!" Grandpa said about the car, a yellow Cadillac old enough to have fins above the taillights but so clean and shiny it looked brand-new.

Only one person around had a car like that: Nando Perez—Lisa's dad, the auto shop owner who had helped the kids with Project Blastoff.

Egg was the first to jump out of the Cadillac, followed quickly by Lisa and her dad, and then . . . eventually . . . Howard.

There were hugs, exclamations, and good feelings all around. Mark gave Howard a playful punch on the arm and asked, "Good to see you, man. I bet you missed Scott, Barry, and me, huh?"

Howard knit his brows thoughtfully, then said, "Not

really." Everybody laughed except Howard, but he didn't seem to mind. Last year when Egg had introduced her friend Howard Chin to the twins, the twins hadn't liked him. He seemed unfriendly. He didn't get jokes. He rarely smiled. It was a while before they realized both that Howard was different, and that different wasn't necessarily bad.

It helped when they found out Howard had his own computer at home, an Altair 8800, and he knew the BASIC programming language. Howard's computer had supported Mission Control for Project Blastoff.

Without him and without it, there was no way the *Crazy 8* spacecraft could have gone into orbit or returned to Greenwood Lake, either.

"What've you people done with Peggy?" Grandpa finally asked.

"My mom's, uh . . . out of town," Egg said. "I talked to her this morning, though. She said she wished she could be here. She said to say hi to everybody."

Meanwhile, Mark was getting impatient. "So what's this surprise, anyway?" he asked. "I think it has something to do with that white thing over by the launch site. Let's walk over and find out."

"Let's drive over," Barry said.

Mark shook his head. "You are as lazy as ever."

"I keep telling you it's not laziness, it's a matter of conserving resources," said Barry.

"Yeah, if you say so," Mark said. "But either way, *I* am walking. Who's with me?"

Everybody was with him, it turned out—even Barry. And as they walked it soon became obvious that Grandpa, Mr. Perez, and the kids from West Milford were having a hard time containing their excitement. Whatever the surprise was, it had to be a doozy.

Barry, Scott, and Mark had found the launch site for Project Blastoff one day the previous August. That morning they had gone rowing out on Greenwood Lake, and they were walking back to Grandpa's cabin for lunch. From the shore of the lake, the path went over a ridge and then down into a scrubby field that a developer had cleared for houses he never got around to building. The field was hard to see from either the lake or the road, and it was further protected on the roadside by a stand of trees.

The boys agreed that the field was perfect for their purposes—especially because it was so close to Grandpa's barn, where the spacecraft was being built. As best they could, the kids modeled the launch site layout after the NASA facility at Cape Canaveral in Florida, only theirs was vastly shrunken and simplified.

In fact, like *Crazy 8* itself, it had had a patched-together look. It was bare dirt, not asphalt, and there were weeds and even tree stumps here and there. The blockhouse that enclosed their own Mission Control had started life as a metal gardening shed, then been wired for electricity and reinforced with cinder blocks to protect from the blast of the rocket. Grandpa had borrowed some orange painters' scaffolding, which they set up next to the rocket to act as a service gantry and provide access to the spacecraft at the top.

Mark hadn't been to the spot in months, but its appearance was permanently impressed on his mind. After all, this was the place where he had spent the most challenging and emotion-packed ninety minutes of his life, ninety minutes during which he had seen his brother launched into the sky and then done everything in his power to bring him safely home.

Now, as he moved toward it through the trees, Mark looked to his right and saw several enormous construction vehicles parked in a row as well as the metal skeleton of a building much larger than the puny blockhouse they had cobbled together. His heart sank.

"Wait—did that developer guy come back to start building the subdivision?" he asked. "Is that the surprise?"

"Not exactly." Egg was grinning.

The path made a sharp curve, and then they emerged from the trees. The area had been paved, and the new building by the construction vehicles appeared to be a hangar, like a garage for airplanes or spacecraft.

But that wasn't the amazing part.

The amazing part was straight ahead, a three-stage

rocket, its bottom and top sections black-and-white, the middle section silver, that rose 150 feet above a steel-framed base. The space vehicle was enmeshed in a web of cables and pipes. Beside was an elaborate orange scaffold, the launch support tower. It was a lot taller and sturdier than the puny structure they had relied on for Project Blastoff.

What they were looking at, in other words, was a compact but up-to-date launch complex—a vision so extraordinary that no one was able to speak for several seconds, not even the locals who had seen it before.

Mark felt as though he had walked from his grandfather's cabin to a sci-fi dream of a space station on an alien planet. Scott was equally overwhelmed, but also the first to find his voice. "Is there an elevator?" he asked.

Egg crossed her arms over her chest and looked at him—disgusted. "Is that all you've got to say? Do you know how hard we worked? Do you even know what that is?"

"I do." Mark's voice quavered. "It's a Titan II rocket, the kind NASA used for the early Gemini missions ten years ago."

"And way, way, way up there"—Barry's voice was a whisper—"that's a Gemini spacecraft, isn't it?"

"It's an Apollo command module," Howard said. "Three seats but without the lunar components. And yes, there is an elevator, Scott."

"Good," Scott said, "because I'd be exhausted if I

had to climb that high wearing a space suit. Those things are heavy."

Now Egg was really annoyed. "Uh, excuse me, but who says *you're* gonna be the one to fly in it?"

Lisa sighed. "Here we go again." Being afraid of small spaces, she was the only one of the kids who didn't want to go into space.

"What . . . ," Mr. Kelly began. "How . . . ? Can someone please . . . ?"

"It's mighty pretty, isn't it?" said Grandpa Joe. "But I wish I'd had your help with getting the permits. It took a lot of fast talking before the town planners were won over. And there may have been some arm-twisting from outsiders, too. Peggy wasn't too free with all the details."

"Do you mind just starting at the beginning, please?" Mom said. "How did this all get here?"

CHAPTER 8

The story was this.

One day soon after Project Blastoff's success, Egg, Lisa and Howard had been sitting together at lunch when they had an idea. It would be dumb if, after all the work they put in, the Greenwood Lake launch site just got overgrown with weeds and brush and disappeared. It ought to be useful somehow, useful for another space mission.

"But we couldn't figure out how to make that happen," said Lisa. "We were busy with school and everything."

"And they couldn't exactly sneak around and operate on their own the way you kids did last summer either," said Grandpa. "After Project Blastoff, everybody knew what they were capable of. If they had started working out here, or borrowing materials, it would have been obvious that something was up."

"So this time we decided to get grown-up help—and grown-up permission—from the beginning," Egg said.

"And they came to me," said Grandpa.

Egg nodded. "You and my mom and Mr. Perez."

Mr. Perez, like his daughter, was a person of few words. Now he smiled.

Grandpa nodded. "And you asked if we, being grown-ups and responsible citizens, would be willing to invite NASA representatives to visit us here for a little confab. Frankly, I'm not sure NASA would have paid any attention to us except that Peggy—Egg's mom—has those connections of hers there."

The grown-ups agreed it would be a shame if the launch site deteriorated. So they issued an invitation. In response, a delegation of NASA officials came to New Jersey and took a tour of the launch site with Mrs. O'Malley, Egg, Lisa, Howard, Mr. Perez, Grandpa, the kids' science teacher, Mr. Drizzle, and one more person. His name was Steve Peluso, and he was a smart kid the West Milford kids knew from school.

Egg didn't like Steve Peluso. She thought he was conceited. Also, he had beaten her out for the blue ribbon at the science fair three years running. Much to everyone's surprise, however, Steve had come through with a key assist on the Project Blastoff mission—an assist that probably saved Scott's life. From then on, even if they didn't exactly accept him as a member of the group, they all agreed they were grateful to him.

"What was it you wanted NASA to do exactly?" Mark asked.

"Develop Greenwood Lake as an alternate launch facility to the one in Florida," Egg said.

"And they did? And this is it?" Mark looked from left to right. "It's practically built already!"

Egg nodded. "We told them putting a new launch complex here would make sense because we had already tested it out once and because, well, not to be all braggy and everything, but—"

"—we're here," Howard said.

Annoyed with Howard for stealing her punch line, Egg narrowed her eyes.

"There is no sense being falsely modest, Jenny," Howard said. "We pointed out that the space program needs to take advantage of every resource, and 'every resource' includes us."

"It's come together so quickly," Grandpa said, "because these characters were here to push the project and to help with construction. Also, we had a bit of luck. A NASA contractor had a Titan rocket in storage in St. Louis. As for the command module, it was a spare used for training. The people at the factory in California shipped it here."

"So what do you think?" Egg asked Barry and the twins.

Scott's and Mark's feelings were conflicted. What they saw before them was awe-inspiring. Huge! Beautiful! Shiny and new!

Looking at it, each boy could almost feel the surging power of that enormous rocket pushing into space.

And each boy fervently hoped that one day soon he would get to feel that power for real.

But the boys both felt something else, too, and Scott tried to explain. "It's beautiful," he said simply. "But I, for one, am righteously, uh"—he looked at his parents, who wouldn't like it if he used the words he was thinking—"*annoyed!*" he said finally.

"How could you do all this without telling us?" Mark asked.

"After all we did together—why would you leave us out?" Barry added.

"The NASA people told us to keep it quiet," Egg said. "In fact, once they grabbed on to our idea, they kind of took over, and they're the ones who told us we couldn't tell anybody else about it yet, not even you."

"So we came up with another plan all on our own," Lisa said. "The idea was this summer when you came back to see your grandpa, we'd show you the launch complex and go to work on some new mission."

Egg added, "It would've been fun, like last year—except even better because now we have experts to help us."

"We felt bad we couldn't tell you yet," Lisa said.

"Some of us, at least." Egg looked pointedly at Howard.

It was quiet for a moment as all this sank in. Then Mrs. Kelly cocked her head. "And now . . . something has happened to change the plan of yours from summer to now?"

"The stranded cosmonaut." Mark looked first at his mom, then his brother.

Scott nodded. "I bet Mrs. O'Malley is in Florida right now. And she's asking NASA to help us use the Gemini spacecraft, and the Greenwood Space Launch Facility, to blast off and rescue Ilya Ilyushin."

CHAPTER 9

The twins figured Egg must know where her own mother was. When she didn't contradict Scott, that meant he was right.

Right?

"While we're here, can we get a tour?" Mom asked. She was looking at Grandpa, but he turned to Egg.

"Jenny's the expert," he said.

"I don't know about that." Egg tried, unsuccessfully, to look modest. "But I'll be happy to show you around."

Like well-behaved students on a field trip, the group bunched up and followed Egg.

"This is our Mission Control building, and Launch Control, too," Egg explained. "NASA has separate facilities, but here at Greenwood they're combined in one."

"Where is everybody, anyway?" Grandpa asked as they walked across the smooth spread of newly laid asphalt. "Usually there's a few NASA guys or some contractors around working, even on weekends."

"I don't know for sure," Mr. Perez said. "But one of their guys told one of my guys at the shop that everybody was all of a sudden recalled to Florida in a hurry."

"Dad!" Lisa said. "You didn't tell me that."

Mr. Perez shrugged. "It didn't come up."

"Why would they be recalled to Florida, do you think?" Scott asked.

"Maybe it has something to do with the cosmonaut," said Barry. "Maybe they have to do extra training to get ready for the rescue."

"If it's training for the rescue, shouldn't we be there?" Mark asked.

That question hung in the air as everyone approached the Mission Control building, which was made of white concrete. Located well away from the rocket, it had been reinforced with heavy blocks and buried partway underground. Egg explained the thick walls had to protect the people inside in case something went badly wrong, which—sometimes—it did.

The Titan that had been used for launching Gemini spacecraft in the 1960s had another use as well. It was a modified ICBM—intercontinental ballistic missile— suitable for delivering a huge bomb to an enemy target.

Compared with the *Crazy 8* team, the U.S. government had tons of money, expertise, and experience. Even so, instead of launching into the air, their rockets sometimes stayed right where they were on the ground and—this was the bad part—exploded.

The entrance to the Mission Control center was down a short, narrow staircase. The only daylight came in from three narrow windows, slits really, on the wall facing the rocket. Egg flipped the light switch to reveal a space that was empty, still, and gray, the kind of space that silenced you the second you walked in.

And then there was all the cool stuff!

Apparently, NASA required a lot more computer power and a lot more equipment for telemetry, tracking, and instrumentation than the *Crazy 8* team had used for their own launch in the fall.

"The equipment in this building is connected to the rocket by a data link," Egg explained. "During launch, closed-circuit TV cameras transmit to the screens you see here."

She pointed to the windows. "They're made of reinforced glass," she said. "For a better view, you have to use that." A heavy-looking, complicated metal contraption with an eyepiece hung from the ceiling. "It's a periscope, like they have on submarines. Maybe you saw the top sticking out of the roof."

As for the furnishings, they were like NASA's

operations in Texas and Florida, familiar to everyone from TV: three neat rows of desks on elevated platforms, each desk with a phone, all of them facing a big screen.

The whole thing had a rough, unfinished look. Here and there lay power drills, sandpaper, and screwdrivers. The electricity to the desks had yet to be hooked up, and wiring spilled from the outlets and electronics like tangled red, white, and black spaghetti.

"What's through there?" Mark gestured at a doorway up five stairs in the windowless back wall.

"Restroom," Egg said, "and a dorm space with two sets of bunk beds in case someone working a long mission needs to crash for a while."

"It feels spooky," Barry said.

"Wait till it's full of people," said Egg.

The next stop was the vehicle assembly building, the one like an airplane hangar. It was as long and wide as a football field, and more cavernous than a cathedral. Inside, the air smelled faintly unpleasant, like cleaning chemicals and fresh cement. Vents high in the walls brought in some daylight.

When Egg flipped switches, a buzz and hum preceded startlingly bright illumination. Intricate webs of scaffolding on either side cast black shadows. Catwalks linked platforms along the distant ceiling. On the concrete floor were stacks of silver storage containers as big as railcars, and orange forklifts parked in rows.

"It sure beats Grandpa's barn," Mark said finally.

"Hey, now," said Grandpa. "I thought the barn worked pretty well for you kids last summer."

"Don't get me wrong. It did," said Mark. "On the other hand, it would be nice to work without worrying a bat might swoop into your hair."

"I'm gonna miss the bats," said Lisa. "This place is so big and clean, it doesn't seem human somehow."

Dad looked at his watch. "Sorry, kids. I had no idea this was going to be quite such a jam-packed visit, and I do have to work tonight. We need to head back on time."

"Okay, so come on, then." Egg herded everyone back outside for the short hike to the main attraction, the one towering over them all—ten stories tall with a spacecraft perched on top.

"Can we go up and take a look?" Scott asked.

"I don't think the elevator's working yet," Egg said.

Howard had been staring upward, arms folded across his chest. "It's kind of disappointing, actually," he said.

"What do you mean 'disappointing?'" Egg narrowed her eyes.

Howard shrugged. "It's not even state-of-the-art."

"Haven't you seen it before, Howard?" Barry asked.

Howard hadn't. In fact, only Egg had seen the rocket on the launchpad. The last time the others had been there, it had still been in pieces on a truck.

Mark looked up. "It's a lot bigger than the *Crazy 8*

launch vehicle, but Howard has a point. The Saturn V that powered the Apollo trips to the moon was more than three times as tall—taller even than the Statue of Liberty. This guy's a pipsqueak by comparison."

"So I guess we won't be taking this one to the moon," Scott said.

Mark said, "Not hardly. I mean, a Titan only produces four hundred and thirty thousand pounds of thrust."

"This Titan does a bit better." Egg's expression was smug. "It's powered by the same superpowerful sugar propellant–based solid fuel as the Drizzle rocket that launched *Crazy 8*."

"How much thrust does it deliver?" Mark asked.

"Not as much as a Saturn," Egg conceded, "but plenty to get the three-seat command module into orbit. Pound for pound, Drizzle fuel is a lot more powerful than the stuff NASA usually uses."

This conversation took place as Grandpa, the Kellys, Barry, Mr. Perez, Lisa, Howard, and Egg walked in a wide circle around the rocket and its support tower. Even if it was small compared to some others, it was an impressive piece of machinery. While both Mark and Scott were disappointed that they couldn't get a better look right now, they were also confident they'd have their chance soon. NASA was bound to assign them to rescue the Russian, right?

And of all the kids on the *Crazy 8* team, they were by

far the best prepared. Hadn't they been reading up on how to fly a spacecraft ever since the fall? Hadn't they done all the simulations together for the last launch? Hadn't Scott himself already been into space?

"Ready to head back for lunch?" Grandpa asked. "I've got sandwiches."

"Don't tell me," Mom said. "Peanut butter and pepper?"

Grandpa shook his head. "Don't be ridiculous. I only make those in summer with peppers from the garden. This time of year, I'm serving peanut butter and mushroom."

CHAPTER 10

Everyone thought peanut butter and mushroom was a terrible idea. Everyone was too polite to say so. Instead, on the walk back to Grandpa Joe's, the conversation was all about the rocket.

"Uh, for those of us who have never built a spaceship," said Mrs. Kelly, "could you guys just say what 'thrust' means again?"

Mark loved any question he knew the answer to. "No problem, Mom," he said. "You know how once there was this guy Sir Isaac Newton who described three laws of motion?"

"I did take science in school, honey," Mom said. "It was a while ago, but we covered Sir Isaac Newton."

Mark said, "Just checking." The truth was that up till they started studying for Project Blastoff, Mark had never heard of Newton's laws himself. But a few trips to the library and one spaceship later, he was pretty knowledgeable on the subject. "The first law says for every action, there's an equal and opposite reaction. A rocket works according to that law. When the fuel burns, gases shoot out in one direction, causing the rocket to react by going in the opposite direction—up."

Mom nodded. "Okay, I get that. And what about thrust?"

"It's a measurement," Mark said, "of how much pushing the fuel does. If you're trying to get something off Earth, you need a lot of thrust. The big thing it has to overcome is the pull of Earth's gravity. But there's also friction caused by the atmosphere, air. How much thrust you need depends on a lot of stuff, but mostly it depends on the mass of whatever you're moving."

"I see," Mom said thoughtfully. "So in that case, the Apollo rockets had to be bigger than the Gemini ones because Apollo carried three people and Gemini only carried two. Apollo had more mass, in other words."

Mark looked uncomfortable. "Uh, Mom? You know how much I hate to disagree with you. . . ."

"Ha!" said Scott. "No, you don't."

"And that *was* very good thinking, Mrs. Kelly," said Egg.

"They're telling you you're wrong, honey," said Grandpa.

"She hates to be wrong," Mr. Kelly said.

"How can I be?" Mrs. Kelly asked. "There were two astronauts in NASA's Gemini program and three in Apollo. It wasn't that long ago. I remember it distinctly."

"That part's right, Mrs. Kelly," Egg said. "But the rocket is lifting tons, so in comparison the extra weight of one single astronaut isn't that big a deal. What's more important was that the Apollo missions had to transport the lunar lander and also something called a service module. So the spacecraft itself wasn't one piece like this one, it was three—and it was more than three times as massive."

"Plus it had to go a lot farther," Scott said. "So it had to carry more fuel, and fuel is heavy too."

"Hmph," Mom said. "How come everybody is smarter than me all of a sudden?"

"It's just something we've studied, is all," said Mark. They were almost back to Grandpa's cabin by this time, and he hurried ahead to open the door and stoke the woodstove. The morning's activities had been so interesting and unexpected that no one had noticed the cold . . . until they went inside, shed their gloves, coats, and hats—and realized how good the warmth of the fire felt.

Grandpa's house consisted of a main room with the woodstove in the middle. On one side was a table with picnic-type benches and a doorway to the kitchen. On the other was a plaid sofa and three mismatched easy chairs rescued from a thrift store. A short hallway led to the bathroom and Grandpa's bedroom.

Overlooking the main room and reached by a ladder was a loft space where the twins slept when they visited. They called it Twin Territory.

"Can I get some help in here?" Grandpa called from the kitchen. "Boys?"

"He means you and Howard," Mark said to Barry.

"I don't think so." Barry grinned.

"Come on, Mark," said Scott. "We've got peanut butter to spread and mushrooms to chop."

In the kitchen, the boys made a happy discovery. While Grandpa really did make peanut butter and pepper sandwiches in summer, he had been kidding about peanut butter and mushroom. Instead, he asked the boys to set out bread, sliced turkey, lettuce, cheese, mayonnaise and mustard so people could make their own lunches.

"I do have mushrooms and peanut butter," Grandpa said after the table was laid. "Should we set those out too?"

"No!" Scott and Mark chorused.

The combination of a hike and excitement had made everybody hungry. Each person fixed a plate and sat down on sofa, chair, or floor in the living room. Meals at Grandpa's were never formal. The twins were just taking their first bites, when the phone in the kitchen rang.

Grandpa groaned. "I'm going to ignore it. I want to eat my lunch in peace, and whoever it is will call back if it's important."

Mark and Scott looked at one another. They guessed Grandpa could do what he wanted about his own phone. . . . But when the ringing persisted for another long minute, everyone except Howard and Grandpa stopped eating.

"Uh, it could be my mom," Egg said at last—and that made Grandpa jump up, go to the kitchen, and answer the phone.

A few moments later, he emerged into the living room, tugging the receiver to the end of its cord. "Jenny?" He held it out. "You were right, it's your mom."

Jenny was already on her feet.

Scott was thinking Mrs. O'Malley must've tried her own house first, then tried here to track down her daughter. The call had to be important.

Mark was trying to remember all he'd read about spacewalking. If he was going to rescue Ilya Ilyushin, a space walk was definitely going to be required.

"Hi, Mom, is everything okay?" Jenny took the phone back to the kitchen. No one was trying to eavesdrop, but she was excited and speaking loudly. "When are you coming back . . . ? Oh, that's good. . . . So what did they say? . . . Wait, what do you mean? . . . But, Mom! I thought . . . No, I do *not* understand, and besides that, neither will . . . Oh, fine. . . . *Fine*, okay? See-you-later-bye."

The next noise was the click of the receiver hanging up.

CHAPTER 11

In the living room, Howard was almost done with his sandwich. No one else was eating. After a long moment, Jenny reappeared in the doorway. She was frowning. "Well, I guess you all heard that," she said.

"What's wrong?" asked Grandpa.

"Is your mom okay?" asked Mrs. Kelly.

"She's fine. She's flying back tonight," Jenny said. "And what's wrong is something I didn't tell you because I wasn't sure. See, I thought probably Mom had gone to Florida to talk NASA into helping us use the Greenwood Launch complex to rescue the stranded cosmonaut."

Mark said, "So didn't she?"

"Yes, but it wasn't the way I thought," Jenny said. "Instead of asking NASA to help us rescue him, she was offering them Greenwood to use for their own rescue."

Mark said, "No fair! The Greenwood Lake Launch Site is ours!"

"Uh, Mark?" Barry said. "Up till a few hours ago, you never even knew it existed."

"Well, yeah," said Mark, "but the point is without us, it wouldn't exist."

"Us and a lot of other people," Lisa reminded him. "If NASA wants to use it, I guess they have a right. It's their stuff out there, isn't it?"

"I'm still mad at my mom, though," Egg said. "I thought she was on our side!"

"Speaking for moms," Mrs. Kelly said, "I'm sure she is, but maybe you kids aren't really best suited for a complicated mission like this? NASA employs professional astronauts. You guys have school to worry about, not to mention chores. And on top of that, you're a bunch of kids."

"I will also speak on behalf of mothers," said Mr. Perez. "They worry. As do fathers. Maybe your mom would like to keep you here on Earth . . . at least until you are a whole lot older."

"On the other hand," said Grandpa, "if I thought my tax dollars were being used to send teenagers to space, I would be proud to pay."

All the grown-ups laughed at this—even quiet Mr. Perez. Meanwhile, Howard asked if there was any more turkey.

"Help yourself," said Grandpa.

Howard got up, made himself a second sandwich, came back to the living room, and sat down. Egg watched him. "How can you even eat at a time like this?" she asked finally. "Don't you care about another space mission? Don't you care about the stranded cosmonaut?"

Howard swallowed. "One thing at a time," he said, "and this is the time for lunch."

"He's got a point," said Barry.

Conversation ceased as everyone followed Howard's lead and finished their sandwiches.

Mark ate too, but without enthusiasm. The crazy emotional ride of the last few hours had dulled his appetite. He'd been thrilled when he saw the new launch facility, angry when he realized he'd been excluded from construction, elated when he thought for sure he was finally going into space.

Now he was disappointed, and it didn't help one bit when his very own brother turned to Egg and said, "I'm disappointed just like you, but don't blame your mom. We've got time for more space missions. The person who hasn't got time is Ilya Ilyushin. As long as someone is going to bring him home—that's the main thing. Right?"

Dad patted Scott on the back. "Well said, son."

Egg said, "I guess."

Mark didn't say anything. His brother was right, of course. But that made things worse. Now Mark was not only disappointed, he was also a bad person for being disappointed.

When had Scott become so good, anyway? Maybe there had been a solar flare when he was in orbit in the fall. Maybe the radiation had affected his brain.

For some reason, this idea made Mark feel better.

Trying to get updates on the cosmonaut and NASA's rescue plan, Mom punched the buttons on the car radio all the way back to West Orange.

But there was no news from NASA, and as for the cosmonaut, the only mentions were continued reassurance from the Soviets that he was in good health and good spirits.

It was the same when the boys checked the late news on TV before bed.

"I don't get it," Mark said to Scott as he pulled up the covers. "NASA has to get it in gear soon. How much breathable air does Ilya Ilyushin have left?"

"Eleven days'—if what the Russians said is right," Scott said.

"Michael's mom says you can't trust them," Mark said. "Would they lie about something like that?"

"How do I know what Russians lie about?" Scott asked.

"You seem to know everything lately," Mark said.

"What's that supposed to mean?" Scott asked.

"Nothing. Shut up so I can go to sleep, would you?"

Scott's attempt to tell his brother to shut up right back got interrupted by a yawn, and soon both boys were asleep.

CHAPTER 12

The next morning, Sunday, Scott Kelly was awakened by a projectile glancing off his shoulder. "Ouch," he said.

"It was only a slipper," Mark said. "And I didn't even throw it that hard."

Scott rolled over and looked at his brother. "What time is it?"

"Early. Come on."

Because of politics in the countries in the Middle East, heating oil had become expensive in New Jersey. The twins didn't understand the connection exactly, but they did know their parents turned the thermostat way down overnight to save money, and their house was chilly in the morning. Now the boys wrapped their blankets around their shoulders and made their way down the hall to the living room, where Mark turned on the TV and began twisting the dial to find the channel they wanted.

Scott had known right away why Mark was waking him up. They had to check the news. Maybe NASA had announced the rescue plan overnight.

At last the dial landed on CBS, which had the earliest weekend news show. There was an item about the Republican presidential primaries and one about how the leader of Cambodia had just resigned and been arrested. Democratic presidential candidates Jimmy Carter and Mo Udall were campaigning in Wisconsin.

Finally, the anchorman said, "Coming up after the break, NASA responds to international humanitarian calls for rescue of the stranded Soviet cosmonaut."

The boys waited eagerly through toothpaste, detergent, and deodorant commercials till at last the news came back. On a screen beside the anchorman was a photograph of smiling guy in a space suit—Ilya Ilyushin—and then that changed and the blue NASA emblem came on.

"Today authorities from nations as diverse as Pakistan, Indonesia, and South Africa are calling for the United States to do something to bring stranded cosmonaut Ilya Ilyushin home," said the anchorman. "In response, the NASA press office has called a briefing.

We take you live to Houston, where a spokeswoman is fielding questions at this hour."

The scene shifted to a woman in a blue blazer behind a podium. A bunch of microphones were in front of her. She looked tired.

". . . unfortunate and tragic situation. At the present time, NASA engineers are assessing the space agency's capacity for mounting a viable rescue operation."

"Is the hang-up engineering or politics?" a voice shouted.

"Can you confirm that the Russian mission has a military component?" another voice shouted.

"Our sources indicate it's biological in nature," said someone else.

Scott thought he wouldn't like it if strangers were yelling at him this early in the morning. Mark just wished she'd hurry and get to the part about Greenwood Lake.

"I have no specifics. For political considerations, you'll have to talk to the State Department. Thank you, ladies and gentlemen. That's all I have to offer at this time."

"That's *all*?" Mark said to the screen.

"That wasn't much!" Scott said.

But the woman gathered up some papers and exited the stage so fast she looked like she might trip on her high heels. Meanwhile, the reporters were as disappointed as the twins. "Whatever happened to détente?" one shouted.

Dad, who had worked a swing shift, four p.m. to eleven p.m., was still asleep, so it was Mom who came in a few minutes later. She didn't even have a chance to say good morning before Mark asked her, "What's détente?"

"Look it up in the—" Mom started to say.

"We already did," said Scott. "The dictionary says 'easing of tensions.' But what's that supposed to mean?"

"Can I get a cup of coffee?" Mom asked.

Scott said, "Sure, Mom."

Mark said, "How long will that take?"

Mom raised her eyebrows.

Mark said, "Sure, Mom."

The boys were way too old for *Captain Kangaroo*, but even so they watched Mr. Greenjeans and Bunny Rabbit dispute the price of carrots for a few minutes while they waited for Mom to return from the kitchen. By this time, Major Nelson had trotted in and made himself comfortable on the rug between them.

"Want to practice some lifesaving?" Scott asked his brother. "Our patient is available."

"No," said Mark.

"What is with you, anyway?" Scott asked.

"I just don't, that's all."

"You're worried you won't get to go up in space and

rescue Ilya Ilyushin and come back down and be a hero, aren't you?" Scott said.

"No," said Mark.

"Yeah, you are. Because I am too. Also, I'm worried about what if we do have to rescue him. Mom and Dad will make me get a haircut for the parade."

Mark smiled in spite of himself. "A haircut will be the least of your problems. That Titan rocket might not be as big as a Saturn, but it's plenty big enough to blow up—*kapow!*" He threw his arms in the air and dropped them to illustrate.

"What is it you're blowing up now?" Coffee mug in hand, Mom came in and took her usual seat on the sofa.

"Nothing, Mom. You know how careful we are," Scott said.

"And let's keep it that way," said Mom. "All right, détente. You know about the Cold War, right?"

Mark was glad to have a question he could answer. "That's how forever the United States and Russia have been enemies without actually shooting at each other."

"Not forever," Mom corrected him. "Since after World War II, the late 1940s. The Soviet economic system, communism, is basically different from ours, capitalism. And their political system doesn't give the citizens the same kind of freedoms ours does. They don't have our kind of real elections, for example.

People aren't allowed to write or say critical things about their leaders."

"Our way is better," Scott said.

"I agree," Mom said. "But if our way is going to work the way it's supposed to, it requires everybody to think and vote and help make good decisions. That's what 'government by the people' means. Maybe in other countries people prefer having leaders who make all the decisions, then tell them what to do—no need to think, no arguing allowed."

"Hey," Mark said, "in that case, life for Scott and me in our house is a lot like living in the Soviet Union."

"Very funny," Mom said.

If it was funny, Scott hadn't noticed. "I remember the protests about the Vietnam War," he said. "They were on TV. Protests are bad, aren't they? And they don't happen in Russia."

"People here are allowed to protest peacefully," Mom said. "The right to assemble is guaranteed in the First Amendment because it's one way for us to tell our leaders what we think. The trouble is when the protests aren't peaceful, when property is destroyed or someone gets hurt."

"So people in the Soviet Union can't protest?" Scott asked.

"Not the same way we can," said Mom.

"Okay, you have totally convinced me," said Scott. "I am never moving to the Soviet Union."

"But what's this got to do with détente?" Mark wanted to know.

Mom sipped her coffee, then frowned, which meant her coffee was cold. She set the mug down on the arm of the sofa. "I'm getting to that," she said. "So the leaders in the U.S. and the Soviet Union disagree about how to run a country, and we don't always trust each other either. At the same time, we are the two most powerful countries in the world, and we both have nuclear bombs. So about six years ago, our two governments decided that we had better find a way to get along or else—"

"*Kapow!*" said Mark, which made Scott laugh and Mom cringe.

Mark said, "Sorry."

Mom continued. "*Not* blowing each other up was something they could agree on, and another thing was not spending all the money they had on building bigger bombs. So since 1969, both countries have been having meetings and writing treaties with the idea that talking is better, and cheaper, than fighting. That deal is called 'détente.'"

"And the Soyuz-Apollo space mission last summer was part of it?" Mark said.

"Yes," said Mom.

"Now the word makes sense," said Scott. "'Lessening of tension' like the dictionary said, making things more peaceful."

"And on TV when that reporter asked the NASA lady about it, he meant it would make things more peaceful if we rescued the stranded cosmonaut," Mark said.

"What NASA lady?" Mom asked.

The boys explained what they'd seen on TV. "And NASA still hasn't promised to rescue the stranded cosmonaut," Mark concluded. "And the whole world wants them to. So they're going to, right? That's what Mrs. O'Malley told Egg yesterday. Isn't it?"

That question was never answered, because the phone rang. Major Nelson, even though he was accustomed to the sound, startled awake and barked.

"It's Egg." Mark looked at his brother. "I'll get it."

"Not if I beat you to the kitchen," said Scott, and the two boys scrambled to their feet.

The boys were right. It was Egg. And by the time Dad came into the kitchen a few minutes later, the phone call was over.

"I don't know why, but I'm in the mood for a cheese Danish!" Dad said heartily, and then he saw glum faces all around. "Uh-oh—what's the matter?"

"NASA isn't going to rescue the cosmonaut at all," Mark said.

"And it doesn't look like the Soviet space program has what they need to rescue him either," said Mom.

"He's got ten days of air left," said Scott. "And after that he'll . . . die."

CHAPTER 13

News outlets all over the world covered the story of the stranded cosmonaut. Every day there were more details about Ilya Ilyushin. He had a wife and a baby. He had two dogs and loved animals. He had been a cosmonaut for ten years.

The twins had never met Ilya Ilyushin, or any cosmonaut, or any Russian person at all—and yet they felt like a friend of theirs had been condemned to a terrible fate.

In West Orange, there was one more week of school before Easter break. Every day that week, they ate lunch with Barry and hatched plans for a cosmonaut rescue. Since the existence of the Greenwood Lake launch complex was a huge secret, they couldn't exactly let other people overhear. So they always sat by themselves at the table known as the "desperation table"—so called because if you were one of the older kids, you had to be desperate to sit there.

The table got its reputation because it was located next to the first graders, and first-grade moms came in to help supervise. These moms were tough. At the desperation table, a single well-aimed spitwad, fake belch, or uproarious joke about sloppy joes would get you sent to the principal's office fast.

The boys were sitting at the desperation table on Tuesday when Scott asked Barry a question about navigation. How did you do it in space anyway? It's not like there were street signs, or even landmarks, like mountains and rivers.

As so often happened, Barry the Brainiac gave Scott a look that implied anyone who didn't already understand something so basic probably also had a hard time tying a shoe, brushing his teeth, or walking.

Barry was eating a tuna sandwich on wheat bread with pickles. Between bites, he turned to Mark. "You understand it, right?" he said.

Mark, mouth sticky with peanut butter, nodded eagerly. "Oh, sure," he said. "Any time I have to perform celestial navigation, I just get out my trusty slide rule and—*bam!*—I'm halfway there."

Barry sighed and wiped his mouth with the back of his hand. "So I guess we start at the beginning. You've heard of triangles?"

"Come on, Barry, we're not *that* dumb," Scott said.

"Good," said Barry, "so how about trigonometry?"

Mark looked at his brother. "Maybe we are that dumb," he said.

Barry checked the clock on the wall. "Okay, I'll try to make this fast. Basically, trigonometry means measuring triangles. But more generally it's using the special properties of triangles to do other things, cool things like mapping the land or the stars or the ocean, or navigating from place to place, or designing roads and buildings."

"Mr. Hackess covered triangles earlier this year," Mark recalled. "There's more than one kind, but the only one I remember is equilateral, where all the sides are the same length."

"The angles are the same too," said Scott, "sixty degrees because the total of all the angles in a triangle has to add up to a hundred and eighty."

Barry nodded. "That's right. And the other triangle types are isosceles, scalene, and right. The last one, the right triangle, is especially useful."

"It's the kind where one of the angles is a right angle, ninety degrees," Mark said.

"A square corner," Scott put in, "like what you want if you're putting up shelves, so nothing rolls off."

"Exactly," Barry said. "Anyway, people have known about the special mathematical properties of triangles at least since the ancient Greeks were alive—more than two thousand years. Astronomers trying to map the sky were the ones who noticed that there's a fixed relationship between the angles of a right triangle and the length of its sides."

Mark and Scott thought that over while Barry ate the last bite of his sandwich, crumpled the wax paper wrapping, and stuffed it in his Star Trek lunch box.

Finally Mark said, "Uh, Barry, could you say that again, maybe using totally different words this time?"

Barry took a deep breath. Apparently, he was trying hard to be patient. "Sure, okay. Uh . . . because of the special properties of right triangles, if you know the length of one side and the size of one angle, then you can calculate the other sides and angles. Those calculations are called trigonometric functions. The functions you hear about most are sine, cosine, and tangent."

"Oh yeah. I hear about them *all* the time," Mark agreed.

"Breakfast, lunch, and dinner," said Scott.

"Lunch at least." Mark held up his sandwich.

Barry sighed. "I'm starting to understand how Mr. Hackess feels trying to teach the two of you. Do you want to understand this or not?"

Mark and Scott said "Sorry" at the same time, then Scott thought of something. "I think I remember something else about right triangles," he said. "It reminded me when you said 'Greek.' Wasn't there some theory some guy with a snake name had . . . a theory that helps you figure out how long the sides are?"

Barry nodded. "You mean a theorem," he said, emphasizing the *m* sound. "And I guess the name Pythagoras—Pi-THAG-or-us—does look a little like python, the snake, when it's written. Anyway, the Pythagorean Theorem says that the square of the hypotenuse is equal to the sum of the squares of the sides."

This time Barry didn't pause to see whether Mark and Scott had understood him. He just went ahead and explained. "So the hypotenuse is the longest side of the triangle, the one that's opposite the right angle. The other two sides are called the legs."

"I really really hate to ask this," Scott said. "But could you maybe use some real numbers as an example? I think it would help me understand."

Barry was always up for numbers, and in a flash he had pulled a pencil from his pocket and was drawing a triangle on a napkin. "I don't have a ruler, so I'll measure with my knuckles, okay? Let's make this leg three knuckles long, and this leg four knuckles." Barry labeled the sides. "So the square of a number is just that number multiplied times itself. You know that, right? So the square of three is nine, and the square of four is—"

"Sixteen knuckles," Mark at least understood this much.

"Right," Barry said. "So what's the sum of nine and sixteen?"

"Twenty-five!" Mark was triumphant. "So according to Pythagoras, this side is twenty-five knuckles long."

Scott looked at the triangle again and made a face. "That can't be right. Just eyeballing it, I can tell it's not nearly that long at all."

"Whoa—cool!" Mark said. "So we're the first ones to figure out Pythagoras was wrong! Maybe kids from now on will study the Kelly Theorem."

Barry's squinched his eyes shut and sighed. "You guys?"

"Oh, shoot—sorry, Barry. You're right," Scott said. "Without you, we never would have recognized our true mathematical genius. The Kelly-Leibovitz Theorem is okay by me. Is it okay by you, Mark?"

Mark nodded. "It's a lot of syllables, but I think we can afford to be generous here."

"*You guys!*" Barry repeated—loudly enough that one of the first-grade moms looked over and shook her head.

Barry mouthed "Sorry" to the mom while Mark and Scott tried hard not to laugh.

"The problem," Barry said quietly, "is you forgot a step. The length isn't twenty-five; the length is the *square root* of twenty-five. According to Pythagoras, the *square* is equal to the sum of the squares, so the length itself is going to be the square root. Get it?"

"And a square root is . . . uh, what, exactly?" Mark asked.

"The number you multiply by itself to get the square," Barry said. "So the square root of nine is three, because three times three is nine. Okay: math problem. What is the square root of twenty-five?"

"Five!" said Scott and Mark at the same time.

"Yes," said Barry, "and at least you're not as dumb as you look."

Mark said, "Thank you."

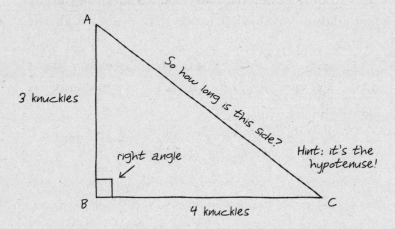

Scott said, "Now that old Greek theorem makes sense. Looking at the lengths of the sides you drew, five knuckles would be right. But how does all this help a guy navigate in space?"

"Well, the fact is there *are* landmarks in space," Barry

said. "They're called stars. And whoever is navigating has a device called a sextant, which does two things. It helps you see stars, and it also measures angles. With the information it gives you, you can use trigonometry to calculate more information—like the distance between you and another star, or another object."

"An object like a Russian space station?" Scott said.

"Just like that," Barry said.

The bell was about to ring, and all three boys crumpled their trash and stood up from the lunch table. On their way out of the cafeteria, Barry nodded sheepishly at the first-grade mom. She didn't seem to be mad, though; she smiled.

"I never saw such an animated discussion about math," she said. "Anybody'd think it was a matter of life and death!"

"Well, it might be, I guess," said Barry.

"But only if we're lucky," said Mark.

CHAPTER 14

On Wednesday, the morning news said that the problem with the Russian space station was related to detaching the Soyuz spaceship that was supposed to ferry the cosmonaut home.

"If we had the blueprints to study, maybe we could make a repair," Barry said at lunch that day.

"But how would we get the blueprints?" Mark said.

"We just need someone at the Russian space center. I think it's called Star City," said Barry. "Or maybe they could mail them to us."

Scott was shaking his head. "Do you know how long the mail takes from Russia to New Jersey?"

Barry shrugged. "I'm not claiming this is one hundred percent realistic. But theoretically, we study the blueprints, we get what we need from Nando's shop, and . . . how many days have we got again?"

"The air runs out in a week," said Mark.

"Right. And we study them, and Scott and I launch on Monday—"

"Wait one minute, what about me?" Mark asked. "There're three seats in that spacecraft."

"We need one for Ilya Ilyushin on the ride home," said Barry.

"Well, I claim one for sure," Mark said. "I have been waiting—"

"Okay, okay, never mind about that part for now," said Barry quickly. "The important thing is I've talked to my brother, Tommy, about the flight characteristics of the Apollo spacecraft, and I've done some calculations. If the information we have about the orbital trajectory of the Salyut is right, we have a launch window of about six minutes on Monday—from 1530 until 1536 GMT."

"Is that when the Salyut will be in orbit over New Jersey?" Scott asked.

"Exactly," said Barry. "For us to get to it is a reasonably short trip, and we won't have to steer too far to the left or right. Once we come up behind it, we can figure out how to travel the last few yards to make the rendezvous. Of course, I'll have to check with Howard on programming the computers so we launch at just the right time."

"Isn't 1500 GMT around 10 a.m. here?" Mark asked.

Barry nodded thoughtfully. "Good point."

"Thank you," said Mark. "Uh . . . why?"

"Well, said Barry, "at that time of day, it could be that the Salyut comes over the horizon with the sun shining on it, but it not being so bright yet. So maybe we'll actually be able to see it. If so, we can use the visual to time our liftoff. There is just one thing we really want to avoid."

"What's that?" Mark asked.

"Bumping into the space station while we're still under rocket power," Barry said.

"You mean *crashing* into it," said Scott.

"That is what I mean," said Barry. "If we do that, then nobody comes home. Oh—and I have another question too."

"Ask Scott," said Mark. "He has *all* the answers."

"Yeah, ask me," said Scott. "Go ahead."

"Fuel usage is a big part of what needs to be sorted out. Do we have enough in our . . . that is, in *NASA's* rocket? And if we don't, can we use the Drizzle fuel from last summer?"

"Sure," said Scott.

"How do you know?" said Mark.

"Uh . . . , I don't actually," said Scott. "But I didn't

want to disappoint him. Look, there's a lot we still have to figure out, right? So, fuel—that's one thing."

Mark looked at his watch. "It is now noon on Wednesday—that's 1700 GMT, right? So you are talking about, uh . . ."

". . . a little less than five days from now," Scott said.

"I don't know about you guys, but I can be packed in five minutes," said Mark.

"Me too," said Barry. "As far as the time line, I don't see a problem."

"Especially since it's only happening in our heads," said Scott. "Why are we even talking about this?"

"We can't help it. We can't stand not doing anything," said Mark.

"Plus we're crazy for thinking we could pull this off," said Scott.

The end-of-lunch bell rang, and the boys grabbed their stuff. On their way to toss their trash, they ran into Michael, the kid whose mom called all Russians commies. "Why have you guys been sitting at the desperation table this week?" Michael asked. "You too good for the rest of us?"

Scott and Mark looked at each other, but Barry spoke first. "We just have stuff to talk about is all. No biggie."

"Oh yeah?" Michael blocked the boys' path. "I bet you're talking about that cosmo-*nut* who's gonna die in space. Good riddance is what I say. One less commie."

This was too much. "You take that back," Barry said.

"I won't," Michael said.

"Grab him!" Mark said.

"*Hey*"—Michael moved out of the way—"three on one's not fair!"

"We'll show you fair," said Scott.

And that's when a volunteer mom stepped in: "What's gotten into you boys, anyway? And sixth graders too! Aren't you ashamed of the example you're setting? No dillydallying now. I want to see you headed for the principal's office. *March!*"

CHAPTER 15

When the door to the principal's office closed behind them, Mark, Scott, and Barry got ready to make heartfelt defenses of their honor and the honor of space explorers in general.

The principal did not want to hear it. Instead, without asking a single question, he gave all the boys three afternoons of detention to be served after Easter vacation.

Then he sent them back to class.

"Are you gonna tell Mom and Dad?" Scott asked his brother on the walk home from school.

"You're the good twin these days. You tell 'em," said Mark.

"Let's put it off till after break," said Scott. "Maybe the school will forget, and we'll never have to tell them."

"Excellent plan," Mark agreed. "I couldn't have thought up a better one myself."

Mom and Dad were almost as upset as the boys about the cosmonaut's situation. But Dad did note one positive. His sons had never before been so well-informed about anything. Every morning, they read the newspaper, and not just the baseball box scores either. Every evening they sat glued to the evening news with Walter Cronkite. Like a lot of people, Dad and Mom called the veteran TV newscaster "Uncle Walt" because no matter how terrible the news was, his consistent manner was comforting.

That night, Scott and Mark watched about half the newscast before Uncle Walt got around to "late-breaking news in the ongoing saga of the cosmonaut with no way home."

Scott and Mark looked at each other. Maybe for once it was good news?

Uncle Walt recapped the story, and then there was video from the network's Russia correspondent reporting from the capital, Moscow. It was so cold there, his breath formed white clouds when he spoke.

"Usually reliable sources in the Russian space agency are saying today that Major Ilyushin is not alone in his plight," the Moscow correspondent said. "Now we want to stress that this is unconfirmed, but our understanding is that the Salyut space station is home not only to the cosmonaut but to several animals as well. It remains unclear for what purpose the Soviets launched the animals into space, or indeed what species of animals they might be."

As for the possibility of rescue by the Soviet space agency, there was nothing new on that. The correspondent did note that the animals might complicate rescue plans if there were any.

"In addition," he went on, "the animals—whatever they are—have their own needs. It's unclear whether officials' previous estimate of resource depletion takes those needs into account."

As usual when the twins watched TV, Major Nelson was dozing between them on the rug. Involuntarily, both boys looked down at him when the report was over. Even though his eyes were closed, Major Nelson seemed to sense their gaze and thumped his tail.

"I hope he's got a dog," Mark said. "A dog would be better company than, like, rats or mice or something."

"What about an ape?" Scott said, and to illustrate he raised one arm over his head, scratched himself, and grunted monkey noises.

Mark replied with his own monkey noises and jungle bird calls too. The noise level caused Mom to call from the kitchen: *"Boys?"*

"Sorry, Mom!" they replied and tried hard to stop laughing.

Finally Mark recovered enough to ask his brother if he knew one of the first Americans in space was a chimpanzee named Ham. "The air force trained him to pull a lever after a light flashed," Mark said. "They wanted to see if he'd be able to do it once he got into space. Back then they thought being in space might make you go instantly insane, since no one had ever gone there before."

"I know, Mark," Scott said.

"Yeah? But did you know he had to train kind of like an astronaut? Anytime he pulled a lever the way he was supposed to, his air force trainers rewarded him with banana-flavored treats."

"I didn't know they gave astronauts banana-flavored treats," Scott said.

Mark ignored this. "And something went wrong with the electrical wiring on Ham's flight, and he kept getting shocks in his feet—poor guy. But even so, he pulled the lever without ever getting a treat, and he splashed down in the Atlantic after sixteen minutes in flight, and he got rescued and was pretty much okay after that. Now he lives in the National Zoo."

Scott said, "Yeah, yeah, I knew all that," which wasn't strictly true, but if he didn't say it, his brother might never shut up.

"Dinnertime!" Mom called from the kitchen. Even though Mom and Dad both had their police jobs, she did most of the cooking. Dad's major contribution was pancakes on weekends.

The whole family was home that night, and Mom had made spaghetti with meatballs. As usual, the boys were starving and dug into their meals as if breakfast, lunch, and after-school snack were only distant memories.

"Really good, Mom," Scott mumbled with his mouth full.

Mark emitted a grunt Mom took to be agreement.

"Thanks," she said. "I was listening to the radio while I cooked. I guess you heard there are now supposed to be animals on board that Russian space station."

"Something to do with germ warfare experiments, I bet," Dad said.

Scott swallowed hard, thinking he'd heard wrong. "What?"

"What the animals are doing there. I bet it has to do with the military. The Russians only went into space in the first place so they could set up a space station and lob missiles anywhere on Earth. You knew that, right?"

"Sure, I knew that," said Mark.

"No, you didn't," said Scott.

Dad reached for the margarine. "That's what the bigwig Soviet leaders wanted, Stalin and after him Nikita Khrushchev, I mean. There were others in Russia, the scientist types, who wanted to go into space to learn more about the universe or just explore—"

On cue, Mark hummed the *Star Trek* theme music, and Scott intoned the show's tagline, "Space, the final frontier."

Dad laughed. "Exactly right. And it's not like our leaders didn't see the military potential, not to mention the spy potential, of having satellites and space stations and giant rockets."

"But I thought the space race between the United States and Russia was just a race to see who would be first to the moon," Scott said.

"That was part of it but not all," said Dad. "It has also been a race to see who could dominate space, another example of the enmity between our two countries."

Scott stopped eating and looked up. "Dad?"

"Yes, son?"

"Is it necessary to turn everything into a vocabulary lesson? I mean, just asking."

"Yeah," said Mark, "what the heck is 'enmity'?"

Dad thought before answering, "Enemy-like feelings. How's that for a definition? Now, who wants more spaghetti?"

CHAPTER 16

On the news the next morning, the stranded cosmonaut came up only once—in a story about Ohio Senator John Glenn. In 1961—fifteen years before—Glenn had been the third American in space and the first to orbit Earth. He was a national hero and a hero to Scott and Mark, too.

The news showed a clip of a speech Glenn had made the day before at a high school in Columbus, Ohio. On a platform flanked by cheerleaders, Glenn said he respectfully disagreed with the government's decision not to help the cosmonaut. "Through my work with NASA and in the senate, I am proud to say I have developed relationships with some members of the Russian space community, and they tell me they would welcome our help. So I say to you, NASA, what's the hold-up?

"The United States of America enjoys unrivaled

technological prowess," he went on. "With that comes
unrivaled responsibility—in this instance the responsibility to reach out the hand of international solidarity to
Major Ilya Ilyushin."

The cheerleaders waved their pom-poms. The audi-
ence whooped and applauded. Glenn said, "I take it you
agree with me?" More waving and whooping. "And you
are not the only ones!" Glenn said. "Today I received a
letter from a little girl, a heartfelt plea in fact, for me to
use what influence I have to encourage our government
to act before it's too late.

"This little girl embodies the American spirit, which
is a generous spirit, and I believe the American people
have spoken!"

Glenn waved; the high school band struck up; Barbara
Walters reappeared, talking about plans for the bicen-
tennial of American independence, which was coming
up in the summer.

Meanwhile, back in New Jersey, Mark Kelly was
finished with breakfast and grabbing his book bag.
"John Glenn should run for president," he said. "What
American wouldn't vote for an astronaut?"

"Yeah—who are you going to vote for for president,
Mom?" Scott was poised by the back door.

It was Mom's day off. She was sitting at the kitchen
table writing out a grocery list. "Our primary's still a
couple of months away," she said. "And it looks like by

then Governor Carter might have the Democratic nomination sewn up. Hey, you two, it's cold out there! Put on your jackets, would you? Why do I have to say that every morning?"

That day at lunch, the twins and Barry sat at their old table in the cafeteria, not the desperation table. This wasn't because of Michael, or because they'd gotten in trouble. It was because by this time they had said all they had to say about rescuing the cosmonaut. Now they were discouraged. Maybe somebody as famous and important as Senator John Glenn could do it, but it looked like a bunch of kids could not.

In the hallway after the last bell rang, the atmosphere was lively and loud. Easter vacation was here at last; the week off stretched luxuriously before them.

"What are you doing over the break?" Barry asked as the three boys merged into the flow of kids heading for the doors.

"Nothing," said Mark.

"Red Cross first-aid class, remember," said Scott.

"Practically nothing," said Mark, "except there'll be chocolate eggs for Easter."

The boys emerged into the weak daylight. It was warmer than it had been that morning but still chilly. They headed down the steps to the sidewalk, where Barry would turn right and Scott and Mark left.

"What's your family doing for Easter, Barry?" Mark asked.

Scott elbowed his brother. "He's *Jewish*, remember?"

"Oops, yeah, sorry," said Mark.

"It's okay." Barry grinned. "Passover starts next week too. I'll take macaroons and kugel over chocolate eggs any day. And since the stuff with Tommy lately, family togetherness is kind of a pain. Way too much eye rolling. Way too much silence."

"Are *you* and Tommy getting along okay?" Scott asked.

"Sure," said Barry. "I don't mind having him around. He's my brother. And what do I care if he gets a job? But I think he and my parents could use a break from each other."

When the twins had left for school that morning, Mom had been sitting at the kitchen table. There were curlers in her hair. She was wearing her bathrobe. When the twins got home from school that afternoon, Mom was sitting at the kitchen table too, only she was dressed and made-up, her blond hair styled and pretty.

Mom wasn't usually waiting for them like this, and right away Scott got a bad feeling. Was something wrong?

"I had a call from the school," she said before the twins even had the chance to grab a snack. "It seems somebody forgot to tell me they had been assigned detention after a little incident in the cafeteria."

"I told Scott to tell you," Mark said. "But he wouldn't."

"That's not true," said Scott.

"And what exactly happened in the cafeteria?" Mom asked.

The twins looked at each other and came to the same conclusion. As a veteran police officer, Mom knew a thing or two about interrogating suspects. She was going to get the truth out of them sooner or later. So, taking turns, they told her what had happened with Michael.

"We didn't like his attitude," Scott concluded. "He's mean."

"And anyway, all we wanted was some privacy to talk at lunch," said Mark. "That's not a crime, is it?"

"No," said Mom, "not according to the penal code of West Orange, New Jersey. But it is a crime to threaten great bodily harm."

"Aw, we wouldn't've hurt him really," Scott said.

"Not too bad, anyway," Mark said.

"And then," said Mom, "there's the matter of not fessing up to your dad and me right away. Honestly, I don't know what's gotten into you two lately. I realize you're upset about the cosmonaut, but it started before that. Would either of you like to comment?"

A long moment passed. Scott looked at a spot on the linoleum. Mark looked out the kitchen window to the empty street beyond.

Mom sighed. "All right, then. I have spoken to your father—"

Uh-oh, thought both boys.

"—and he agrees with me that the best treatment for whatever's ailing you is a stay with your grandpa during the school break."

The April afternoon had been gray and damp. Now it was as if bright sunshine filled the room.

"For real?" said Mark.

"When do we leave?" said Scott.

"Dad's and my work schedule is packed," said Mom, "and Grandpa's truck is in the shop. It looks like we'll all have to put up with each other till at least Monday."

Mark saw this delay as a dark cloud over his sunshine. "I have an idea," he said. "Can Barry come with us, do you think? He's lazy, but even so, Grandpa likes him. If Barry came, then maybe Tommy could drive us."

Knowing the way Mom's mind worked, Scott jumped in. "It'd be a favor to Barry, and his family, too," he said. "Barry says they're not getting along so well lately."

Mom shook her head and sighed. "What a shame after all they've been through. Let me give your grandfather a call."

....

CHAPTER 17

Mr. and Mrs. Leibovitz readily agreed to let Tommy drive the boys to Grandpa McAvoy's house. They even lent him the family car, a roomy Chevrolet Caprice that had a plush interior, whitewall tires, and a factory-installed stereo tape deck.

As Tommy steered the big car onto Highway 280 the next morning, Saturday, his passengers were feeling optimistic, their previous discouraged mood forgotten. They hadn't said a word about it yet, but Barry, Mark, and Scott were all thinking more or less the same thing: At Greenwood Lake, a perfectly good rocket awaited, and so did a perfectly good launch facility.

Weren't they just begging to be put to use?

Tommy tuned the car radio to a rock station. On the hour, the DJ read the weather forecast: "We're looking at a high of fifty this afternoon, while tomorrow, Sunday, temps will hit a balmy sixty-three degrees. Monday we welcome back winter with a high of only forty-five under partly cloudy skies."

From the backseat, Scott piped up. "How cloudy is 'partly cloudy,' do you think?"

Barry was riding shotgun. "I looked in the paper this morning," he said. "If the ceiling stays at 2,000 feet like they predict, it'll be decent launch weather."

Scott started to ask another question, but Tommy interrupted. "Wait, wait, wait—*whoa!*" He looked from Scott to Mark in the rearview mirror. "Are you talking about that cosmonaut guy? Are you crazy?"

Scott grinned. "*Crazy 8*, that's us."

"Project Blastoff seemed impossible too," Mark said. "But we pulled that off. This time will be even better because we have experience. Plus we don't have to build our own spaceship."

"There's something else, too," Barry added. "Project Blastoff was just a cool thing to do over the summer and a science fair project for Egg. Now a person's life is at stake."

Tommy inhaled a long breath and let it out again. "Ye-e-a-a-ah," he agreed, "but what about *your* lives?"

"We'll be extra careful," said Mark.

"We promise," said Barry. "Oh, and don't say anything to Mom and Dad, okay?"

"You don't have to worry about that," Tommy said. "I don't think Mom and Dad are speaking to me."

For a few miles, they all listened to the radio, looked out the windows, and thought their own thoughts. Finally, Tommy spoke again. "Not that I'm necessarily on board with this idea, but let's say someone we know *was* to fly to the cosmonaut's rescue—who would it be?"

The three boys all answered at once, "Me!"

Tommy laughed. "Hope you've got a nice, big spacecraft. You'll need room to bring back your Russian passenger too."

Scott knew discussing who got to fly would only end in an argument, an argument he wanted to put off as long as possible. So he changed the subject. "I've been wondering something. The Soviets launch from someplace called the Baikonur Cosmodrome, right? Where is that, anyway?"

As usual, Mark was ready with the answer. But Tommy was even faster. "It's in a region of the Soviet Union called the Kazakh Republic. It's mostly desert, the middle of nowhere."

"Yeah, that's right," said Mark.

"How do you get there?" Scott asked.

Mark looked at his brother. "Are you planning a field trip?"

Scott shook his head no. "I'm just thinking it would be good if we had somebody on the ground there, somebody to coordinate our mission with the Russians. They could show us blueprints of the Salyut, get us in radio contact with Major Ilyushin, pinpoint the orbit of the Salyut, that kind of stuff."

"Heck, no problem, then," said Mark. "All we need is somebody who totally understands the math, science, and engineering, and also talks Russian."

The twins saw Barry and Tommy exchange glances, then Barry said, "Actually, I speak a little Russian."

"No way," said Mark.

"Our grandparents emigrated from Russia," Tommy explained. "Before she died, our grandma taught Barry. She tried to teach me, too, but I was a lousy student."

"Say something in Russian, Barry!" Scott said.

"Uh . . ." Barry thought for a minute. *"Poyadyte ikru, poshalusta."*

Mark nodded. "Yeah, that's Russian, all right."

"How do you know?" Scott asked.

"'Cause I didn't understand it, and I don't understand Russian," Mark said. "What did you say, anyway, Barry?"

"'Pass the caviar, please,'" Barry said.

"Yuck!" said Mark. "Isn't caviar made of fish eggs or something?"

Barry shrugged. "All I know is Grandma told me Russians like it."

"I'm not sure that sentence will be useful when you're talking about rockets," Scott said.

"It's better than you can do," Barry said. "And anyway, it's not like I could really go. I've got some money saved, but not enough for a plane ticket."

"Plus you'd have to have a passport," Mark said.

"That I've got covered," Barry said. "My family went to France last year, remember? My passport's still good."

"Actually," Tommy said, "you don't want to go to Kazakhstan anyway. That's where the launch site is, but the control center is closer to Moscow. I think the base is called Star City."

Announcing that they needed gas, Tommy steered the car off of the highway and into a service station, where an attendant filled the tank.

"Fifty-seven cents a gallon!" Tommy said. "I can't believe it's so expensive."

"While we're here, let's take a restroom break, okay?" Tommy said.

The boys piled out of the car. A few minutes later, Scott looked around and saw Tommy a short distance away, smoking a cigarette. "I didn't know your brother smoked," he said to Barry.

"Usually only when he's nervous about something," Barry said.

"What's he got to be nervous about?" Scott asked.

Barry shrugged. "I don't know. I thought he was feeling pretty good today. He's glad to be out of the house."

Back on the highway, Barry asked his brother if

everything was okay. Tommy nodded, but the twins could see in the mirror that he was frowning. Finally, Tommy said, "I'm thinking about something is all. Look, are you guys serious about this deal—this rescue deal?"

"Yes," Mark said. Scott and Barry nodded.

"And, Barry"—Tommy looked at his brother—"would you really go to the Soviet Union if you could?"

Something about the way Tommy asked that question made Mark's heart bump. It was one thing to contemplate going up in space. They had done that before—or at least Scott had. But going to the Soviet Union? For real? And the way Tommy had asked the question, Mark could tell he wasn't just fooling around.

For several moments it was quiet. Then Barry took a breath and said, "*Da.*"

Scott and Mark looked at each other. *Huh?* In the mirror, they saw Tommy grin.

"That's Russian for 'yes,'" he said. "Even I got that far with Grandma's lessons. Look, Barry, I've got an air force buddy from Vietnam who owes me a favor, and the U.S. military has bases all over the world. He won't be able to fly you direct to the Soviet Union, but I bet he can get you close."

CHAPTER 18

At Grandpa Joe's house, a welcoming committee awaited. The rest of the *Crazy 8* crew was there and so was Egg's mom, Mrs. O'Malley. She shook hands with Tommy and greeted Barry and the twins with a big smile. Scott and Mark smiled back, but their emotions were all mixed up. Mrs. O'Malley was the mother of their good friend, after all, and usually they liked her fine. Now, though, they saw her as the major obstacle between them and their plan to rescue Ilya Ilyushin.

It was too early for lunch, but Grandpa had bought doughnuts. Happy as they all were to see one another, the conversation between bites was quieter than usual. Finally Mrs. O'Malley brought up the topic on all their minds. "Look, I know you're unhappy that NASA isn't sending you to bring back the stranded cosmonaut—"

"Us or anyone else, either," Egg said.

Mrs. O'Malley looked at her daughter and sighed. "We've been through this already, Jenny. There are political and international considerations that you kids can't possibly understand."

Egg said, "We understand one thing, Mom. That poor man is stuck and is going to die, and no one will help him. That's wrong."

"Now, Jenny," Grandpa started to say, "your mother—"

But Mrs. O'Malley interrupted. "It's okay, Joe. The truth is I am disappointed too. I think NASA and our government have made the wrong call here. But something you learn as you get older is to accept life's disappointments and move on."

Scott thought this over before filing it under another of his mental categories: Advice to Consider . . . Just As Soon As I Get Old.

Grandpa looked at his watch. "I've got to pick up my truck from Lisa's dad's shop," he said, "and Peggy here, Mrs. O'Malley, has generously offered to drive me. Tommy, will you still be here when we get back?"

Tommy looked at Barry, then the twins. "Uh . . . it depends," he said finally. "I might be meeting up with an old air force buddy."

"Bring him over! The more the merrier," Grandpa said. "We'll be back as soon as we can. In the meantime, kids, remember: Don't blow anything up."

This made everybody smile. During the time they were working on the *Crazy 8* spacecraft, practically every grown-up who heard about it gave them that same warning. After a while, it had become a joke.

Mark waited until he heard the car start before making his announcement: "Barry's going to Moscow."

Egg nodded. "Good. Have you worked out the logistics?"

"Thanks to my brother here," Barry said. "It looks like I can fly from McGuire Air Force Base to the U.S. Army airfield in Stuttgart, West Germany. After that it's a short flight to Bern, Switzerland, and a straight shot to Moscow."

"That doesn't sound very easy," said Scott, "or safe, either."

"On the other hand, it's probably safer than launching in a rocket ship," Mark pointed out.

One by one, the kids wiped the doughnut crumbs from their lips and took seats. Lisa pulled out a pad of paper and a pen. "McGuire is the base near Trenton, right?" she asked.

"That's the one," said Barry.

Still on his feet, Tommy looked from one kid to another. "Wait a second," he said. "How come Jenny knew right away what Mark was talking about? Do you all have some kind of telepathic communications link or something?"

Howard raised his eyebrows. "There is no such thing as a telepathic communications link, so how could we have one?"

"Aw, come on. You know what I mean," said Tommy.

Howard shook his head. "No, I don't."

"It's not telepathy, Tommy," Egg said. "It's just we worked together so much last year that each of us can kind of predict what the others are thinking."

Lisa said, "Like, I bet Scott and Mark and Barry spent every day at lunch this week trying to come up with plans for rescuing Ilya Ilyushin."

"We sure did," said Mark.

"Egg, Howard, and I did the same thing. And now"— Lisa held up her pen—"it's time to write down what we've got figured out so far. Only we have to hurry so we get it done while the grown-ups are out of the way."

Tommy smiled. "At least you didn't include me with the 'grown-ups,'" he said, "and I guess I've got an urgent phone call to make."

Scott told him there was a phone in Grandpa's bedroom; Tommy left to make the call. Mark looked around the table. "All right, let's do this. Assuming Tommy's buddy comes through, there's still a hole in Barry's plan. Where is Star City exactly, anyway?"

"That's top secret," said Mark.

"I have an idea," said Egg. "Did you happen to hear John Glenn on the news yesterday?"

Mark and Scott nodded. Barry said, "He mentioned some kind of back-channel communications with the Soviet space agency, right?"

Egg smiled. "Yeah, he did. And guess what? *I've* got my own back-channel communications—with Senator Glenn's office."

A goofy thought entered Scott's head. "You're not the 'little girl' he talked about on TV, the one who wrote to him?"

Egg looked embarrassed. Lisa laughed. Even Howard cracked a smile.

"I *was* pretty insulted," Egg said. "I am a perfectly normal-size preteen. But the important part is that after the letter, a lady on his staff called me back. She recognized my name from news stories about *Crazy 8*. She said the senator wants to help the cosmonaut too, and he might be willing to help us. We just have to keep his name out of it. He's interested in the vice presidential nomination, and he doesn't want controversy."

Scott's eyes were wide. "You're saying we've got *John Glenn* on our side?"

"We can't miss!" said Barry.

"Egg, you've got to call the lady as soon as Tommy is done with the phone," Mark said. "See if John Glenn's Russian connections can help us with Barry's travel."

Egg looked at Mark. "Excuse me? Was that a request?"

"My brother means well," Scott said. "But sometimes

his 'leadership potential' looks like plain old bossiness. Maybe we should start calling him 'bossy-pants.'"

"We don't have time to fool around," said Mark. "And I don't need a nickname," he added.

"So I'm the only one who gets a nickname around here?" Egg asked.

"Yes, because you deserve it and you are an egghead," said Mark.

"And we mean that as a compliment," Scott added.

Before Grandpa Joe and Mrs. O'Malley returned, the *Crazy 8* crew made a plan for their rescue mission, outlined job responsibilities, and thoroughly busted Grandpa's budget for long-distance telephone calls.

"It's okay," Mark reassured everybody. "He won't get the phone bill till this is all over, and by then we'll be heroes—provided the whole thing works out."

"What if it doesn't work out?" Howard asked.

"You mean like if something bad happens to Ilya Ilyushin when we're trying to rescue him, and the Soviet Union gets mad and starts a war?" Scott said.

Howard nodded. "Like that."

"In that case, we'll have more important things to worry about than Grandpa's phone bill," said Scott.

By now the kids and Tommy were standing by the front door. Barry had his duffel bag over his shoulder.

Packed for a week at Greenwood Lake, it would also serve for a week in the Soviet Union.

"I hope there's a Laundromat," Egg said.

Barry said, "One that takes nickels instead of, uh—"

"Rubles," Mark said.

"How did you know that?" Scott asked his brother.

Mark shrugged. "I know everything."

The lady in John Glenn's office had told Egg she would get right to work on the Russia part of the trip. Egg had given her Tommy's buddy's number. The lady was going to phone him when she had the details worked out. Now there was no time to waste, and everyone knew it.

Even so, they put off saying good-bye.

"Total flying time—Germany to Switzerland to Moscow—is about twenty hours," Tommy said. "I don't know for sure how long it will take to get to Star City, but an hour or longer."

"So you'll be there Sunday sometime?" Mark said. "And so we can launch on Monday."

"Yes, depending on how much time he spends shopping for chocolate in Switzerland," Tommy said.

"What else do they eat in Switzerland, anyway?" Barry asked. "I like chocolate—but I can't live on it."

"I hear the goat cheese is good," said Tommy. "Cheese and chocolate—you should be okay with that."

"It's going to be awfully cold in Moscow," Lisa said.

"How do you know?" Egg asked.

Lisa shrugged. "I read this book about the Russian space program. Have you got a coat, Barry?"

Barry shrugged. "A Windbreaker."

Scott reached for the coat hooks by the door. "You'd better take this." He grabbed one of Grandpa's heavy fleece-lined jackets. "Grandpa won't mind, provided you're back before next winter."

Barry was zipping up the jacket when everyone heard a familiar sound—tires on gravel.

Egg pulled the curtain aside. "Shoot! Mr. McAvoy's back early!"

Scott pushed open the front door. Mark put his hands on Barry's shoulders and shoved. "Hurry up and get going! Wave good-bye; don't stop to talk! We'll think of some way to explain. Now, *move!*"

CHAPTER 19

Coming up the walk, Grandpa looked over his shoulder at the Chevy Caprice retreating toward the highway in a cloud of dust. "Jenny's mom will be here soon. She stopped to pick up subs—and how come Barry's taking off in such a hurry wearing *my* winter coat?"

"He'll bring it back," Mark told his grandfather. "And, uh . . . they said to say good-bye."

"And thanks," said Lisa.

"Everything's totally fine," Scott added.

The subs were a special treat from the best deli in town, but the kids wolfed them down so fast they hardly tasted them. The first one done eating, Mark slurped the last of the Coke-flavored ice, crumpled his napkin, and jumped to his feet.

"That was delicious," he said to Mrs. O'Malley. "Thank you. Uh . . ." He looked at his friends. "Do you guys want to take a walk or something?"

If Grandpa and Mrs. O'Malley thought this was an odd choice of activity, they didn't say anything, and what's more, they offered to clean up after lunch. Five minutes later, Egg, Mark, Scott, Howard, and Lisa were walking briskly down the path toward the Greenwood Lake launchpad.

"It feels weird not to have Barry here," Scott said.

"It is more than just weird," Howard said. "I can't propagate the trajectories, program the guidance and navigation systems, and figure out the fuel requirements by myself. With Barry gone, I am going to need help."

"Why didn't you say that before?" Mark asked him.

"It was so obvious I thought you knew. We need somebody else with Barry's skills," Howard said.

"I'm good at math and science," said Egg.

"Me too," said Lisa.

"I know that, but you have your own jobs," Howard said.

"Also, I'm still planning on being an astronaut this time," said Egg.

"We all are," said Howard.

"Speaking of being an astronaut—" Mark began.

Scott held up his hand. "We are not having this discussion now."

"We probably need to have it before we actually launch," Egg said.

"Yes, but not now," Scott said, "because now we are solving the problem of Howard needing help. And unless I'm missing something, we have only one alternative."

Everybody knew what the alternative was, and nobody wanted to say it in front of Egg. For a few moments, the only sounds were footsteps on the hard dirt path and the breeze rustling the needles in the evergreens. Then Scott said, "He saved my life," and Howard said, "He's really smart," and Lisa said, "He's not that bad."

Egg closed her eyes and counted to ten. Her expression was pained. "All right. All right." She surrendered. "I will call Steve Peluso."

Egg was as good as her word. When they reached the Mission Control blockhouse, she went inside to call while everyone else assessed the progress made since their last visit. New black asphalt had been smoothed into place between the vehicle assembly building and the rocket. The elevator in the support tower was operational. Back inside, the wiring on the consoles was complete.

"What did he say?" Scott asked Egg after she hung up.

"He said he can help us, but not till Monday," Egg said.

"I hope he learns fast," said Scott.

"Okay." Mark took a breath and looked at the others. "We have to stay focused. What do we need for launch?"

"Two astronauts," Egg said.

"One rocket," Scott said.

"Computers. Radios. Mission Control," Howard said.

"Snacks for the astronauts," Mark said. "Whoever is going will be gone longer than Scott was. How long do you think, Howard?"

"We won't know the Salyut's precise location and overflight time until we hear from Barry. So then we'll have a very accurate launch time, I hope. And then there is how long this entire thing is going to take in space. I think we are looking at less than twenty-four hours, but if things don't go well it could be several days."

"This time we put the food in tubes the way NASA does," said Scott, "so it doesn't float all over the place and gum up the equipment."

"Where do you get food in tubes?" Mark asked.

"I have an idea for how to do it," said Lisa. "Just don't expect McDonald's, okay?"

"What about a first-aid kit? Like we have in Red Cross class?" Scott asked.

Egg laughed. "Now I'm picturing teeny tiny bandages for guinea pigs and mice, and teeny tiny oxygen masks too."

Lisa said, "*Skylab 3* carried spiders on board, remember? They wanted to see if the spiders would spin webs in space, and they did."

"We are *not* rescuing any Russian spiders," said Mark, "or snakes, either."

"You guys"—Lisa frowned—"I think there's something we're forgetting. How do you picture our astronaut, whoever it is, going about this rescue, anyway? It's not like we can dock the Apollo spacecraft to the Salyut. Our hardware doesn't match up with theirs."

"Of course not," said Mark. "So what we have to do is station our Apollo capsule as close as possible to the Salyut without colliding. Then one of us performs an EVA. EVA stands for 'extravehicular activity,' also known as a space walk."

"We know what it stands for, Mark," said Scott.

"Just being sure," Mark said. "Anyway, then I . . . that is, the astronaut, floats on over and knocks on the hatch. The Salyut is in a stable orbit right around 220 miles above Earth. And since both spacecraft are in freefall, orbiting around Earth, we float."

Scott said, "We know that, too."

Mark kept talking. "By then, we hope Barry and his new Russian pals will have warned Major Ilyushin to expect company. He depressurizes the Salyut and opens the hatch. Our guy enters via the airlock, assesses the situation, and—probably—floats on back with Major Ilyushin." Mark shrugged. "Easy-peasy."

"Except for one thing," said Lisa. "Our astronaut, whoever it is, will be wearing a space suit. Right?"

Mark and Scott looked at each other, then they looked at Lisa. What was with her, anyway? She was smart, plus she could do practical stuff like welding. Without Lisa, the *Crazy 8* spacecraft never would have been built. So how come all of a sudden she was talking like some kind of airhead *girl*?

Of *course* an astronaut on a space walk would have to wear a space suit! Cosmonauts have to wear them too.

There was no atmosphere to breathe in outer space, no pressure to keep the moisture in the human body or the nitrogen in the blood from vaporizing and expanding. Without the protection of a space suit, the cells in your body would be exposed to the vacuum of space, the sun's radiation would fry you, your blood would boil, your eyes would pop out of your head, and then you'd freeze in the darkness because there was no atmosphere to conduct heat and keep you warm.

Neither Scott nor Mark wanted to be sarcastic and hurt Lisa's feelings. It was Scott who spoke, gently and patiently. "Yes, Lisa. On a space walk, you have to wear a space suit."

"Okay," said Lisa, "and where do we get a space suit by launch time? The kinds of fancy materials we need are not available at any old fabric store. What Scott wore on *Crazy 8* was only a flight suit. It didn't have nearly the protection you'd need in outer space, or its own oxygen supply either. Also, what about helmets?"

Scott opened his mouth to answer before realizing he

had no answer. Mark's dream of floating in star-studded space evaporated.

Howard scratched his head. "That's a problem."

But Egg was unfazed. "Come on." She pointed toward the Titan rocket. "Let's take an elevator ride. NASA has helpfully provided us with a whole lot of fancy technology. It could be they left some space suits, too. And if so, I think I know where they are."

CHAPTER 20

There was nothing fancy about the elevator car, a plain metal box at the core of the launch support tower, itself more of a tall skinny skeleton than a building.

"Going up?" Mark asked, his finger poised to press a button.

"Yes, please," said Egg. "Tenth floor and step on it."

On the clattering ride, the kids watched the shiny skin of the rocket slide by. At the top, the doors opened to a gangway. Trying not to look through the open metal grid to the ground below, they crossed it and passed through a door to a small white room where astronauts, helped by technicians, made final preparations before climbing into the spacecraft.

Egg looked the white room over and announced it reminded her of their mudroom at home, only no washer-dryer and no wallpaper; in fact no decoration of any kind. A ventilation duct snaked from ceiling to floor; electrical cables lined the walls. Opposite the elevator was the steel and aluminum hull of the Apollo command and service module (CSM) itself.

To the left was a gray control panel packed with buttons, levers, and dials. Its top portion was a wall clock that showed the time as seven twenty-seven. The time in New Jersey was two twenty-seven in the afternoon, but scientists all over the world synchronize their clocks with the time at the Royal Observatory in Greenwich, England. It's known as Greenwich Mean Time, and in the spring it's five hours ahead of Eastern Standard Time in the United States.

Lining the right-hand wall were metal storage lockers, gray like everything else. While Egg and Howard opened them one by one and rummaged inside, Scott and Mark tried to rotate the handle on the heavy mechanism that opened the hatch to the crew compartment of the CSM.

"Can we get some help here?" Mark asked.

"No time for that now," Egg said. "Come and help us look for space suits."

For a few minutes, it was quiet but for the metallic *squeak* and *crack* of locker doors opening and closing. Then Howard straightened up and asked, "Is this what we are looking for?" On Howard's face was his usual slightly puzzled expression. In his arms was a white space helmet with the blue NASA emblem printed on the side.

"Woo-hoo!" Egg said. "I thought so."

Mark grinned.

Scott said, "Is there another one? And what about suits?"

Within a few minutes, the kids had found two more helmets and three space suits as well—enough to outfit a three-man Apollo crew. The suits were big and bulky, and it seemed to take most of Scott's strength to hold one up by its shoulders.

"I didn't know it'd be so heavy!" he said.

Mark tugged it away from his brother. "Oh it can't be that," he started to say, but when he felt its full weight, his knees bent. "Heavy," he grunted.

"It won't weigh a thing in microgravity," said Egg.

"What's it made of, anyway?" Scott asked. He expected Mark would answer, but for once, his brother's face was blank.

It was Lisa who told them about the suits. They were made of many layers, rubber on the inside to contain the pressurized oxygen that kept the astronaut alive, netting to help the rubber keep its shape, sheets of foil-like Mylar for extreme temperature and radiation protection, a tough layer of felt to protect against pea-size meteorites, and an outer covering of white nylon.

"Pea-size meteorites?" Mark said. "What about baseball-size ones?"

"Those you have to duck," Lisa said. "No suit could protect you from them. But don't worry. They're not that common. Oh—and one more thing. The pants used for the EVA have extra insulation made out of fiberglass," Lisa said. "The idea is so you don't get burned by the nitrogen jets on the AMU."

"What's an AMU?" Mark asked.

"Write this down, everybody," Scott said. "Two things in a row my brother doesn't know."

"I *will* know as soon as you let Lisa answer the question," Mark said.

"Astronaut maneuvering unit," Lisa said. "It's like a jetpack, only with twelve tiny rockets pointing in all directions to move you around without the need for an umbilical—a cord that connects you to the ship. They're still pretty experimental, but useful for rescue. That's one of the reasons they were designed."

Mark, Scott, and Egg all spoke at the same time: "*Cool!*"

Lisa, the only one of them uninterested in being an astronaut, shrugged. "If you like that kind of thing."

"There's one more thing I don't understand," Scott said. "Where did these suits come from? I thought NASA custom-made them for each astronaut."

"*Ew*, you mean these must be used?" Mark said.

"From the NASA thrift store," said Egg.

"I don't think so," said Lisa. "Every astronaut got

three, one for flight, one for training, and one as a backup. I don't know who these were made for, but I bet they're backups."

As best they could in the small space, the boys and girls separated to try the suits on for size. Howard and Egg went first. They found that the space suits felt rubbery, like the skin of an inner tube, and even after the fasteners were tightened and zippers pulled up, they sagged like loose skin on an elephant.

"Is this how it's supposed to be?" Howard asked.

"It's not pumped up yet—pressurized, I mean," Lisa explained. "In space, you're going to look like a snowman."

CHAPTER 21

Space suits were never designed to be worn on planet Earth. They were huge, hot and in every way uncomfortable. The fish bowl helmets, heavy and hard, were even worse.

"My nose itches!" Scott complained when at last it was his turn and the helmet had been securely locked to its neck ring. "How am I supposed to scratch my nose?"

"Is this thing air-conditioned?" Mark wanted to know.

Egg looked at Lisa. "I think they're talking."

It was hard to tell. The helmets had big visors that protruded over the faceplates, putting them in shadow, and the faceplates themselves were like dark glasses, tinted to provide sun protection.

"I guess we still have to figure out the fine points of how you work these things," Lisa said. "There's a microphone and earphones too, but I don't know which switch turns that all on. Anyway, we don't have the radios hooked up." She knocked on the side of Scott's helmet. "Hello-o-o in there! How does it fit?"

Scott shrugged and shook his head. He could see Lisa was talking, but he had no idea what she was saying. Meanwhile, Howard had been studying the outside of Mark's suit inch by inch. The hoses for the oxygen came together in a pack on the chest. "How do we turn it on?" he asked. "It's suffocating in there. They're going to need to breathe soon."

These words were hardly out of his mouth when both Scott and Mark lifted off their helmets and took big gulps of air.

"So how was it?" Lisa asked.

"Great," Scott said.

"Fits perfect," Mark said.

After their turns, Howard and Egg had said more or less the same things, more or less unconvincingly.

Lisa laughed. "You guys remind me of Cinderella's stepsisters with the glass slipper. They wanted to marry the prince. You want to go up in space."

"That suit *was* pretty big on you, Egg," Mark said.

"I can tuck the pant legs into the boots," Egg said.

Howard was the tallest of the five of them. "I won't even have to do that," he pointed out.

"If we're going by who the suits fit best, then Scott

and I are obviously Cinderella," said Mark.

Scott looked at his brother. "You know something? 'Cinderella' is one name I never expected you to call me."

"Oh, you know what I mean," said Mark. "We're the closest to being the right size for the suits. We're not as tall as Howard but not as skinny, either. And, Egg, sorry, but you're too small."

Lisa shook her head impatiently. "If you're looking for the best way to decide who flies, the suits aren't it. They're going to have to be adjusted for whoever flies. I think we can do it with straps and Velcro and maybe some duct tape."

"Look, the time has come," Mark said. "We have to decide who's going. We can't put it off anymore."

For a few moments, it was quiet as everyone seemed to look at everyone else—sizing up the competition. They were all stubborn and determined. They had all worked hard. None of them wanted to back down . . . but finally Egg did. She sighed. She slouched. She straightened up. She turned to Howard and sighed again. "We have to let *them* go—Scott and Mark, I mean."

Howard's accustomed expression, puzzlement, turned to surprise, then irritation. "No, we don't!" he insisted. "It's not fair. Scott has already been in space!"

Egg nodded sadly. "Believe me, I know. And I'm sorrier than you, if that's possible. But when Tommy took us to the amusement park last summer to do the testing for *Crazy 8*, it was Scott and Mark who did the best. Remember how you felt when you were riding the roller coaster? And don't forget, Scott has some experience at this. None of the rest of us do. And on this mission we have to get it right or that poor cosmonaut dies. This is really serious"

Howard made a face. "I remember."

"And riding a rocket into space is going to feel the same, or worse," Egg said. "Isn't that right, Scott?"

Scott nodded. "Yeah, your stomach definitely jumps around as the g-forces change."

"What if one of us felt sick and couldn't do the job, couldn't help Ilya Ilyushin?" Egg asked. "And besides, for his sake, for the sake of the mission, it's probably *good* that Scott has experience. You and I, we have to be unselfish about this, Howard. Even if"—she narrowed her eyes at Scott—"it isn't fair."

Mark was grinning broadly. "I vote with Egg."

Lisa looked at Howard's glum face. "Howard?" she said gently. "You know you can't quit, right? Even if you're disappointed?"

Howard looked up, and his usual, slightly puzzled expression was back. "Who said anything about quitting?" he asked. "You guys couldn't do this without me."

"Good man." Mark slapped him on the shoulder.

"Ouch." Howard rubbed his shoulder.

Scott, meanwhile, was impressed with what Egg had

done. She gave up something she really wanted because she thought it was best for somebody else, somebody she didn't even know. Was he capable of being that unselfish?

He wasn't sure.

Of course, he would never in a million years say any of that out loud—especially to a girl. That would just be weird.

Before the kids said good-bye that afternoon, Egg gave them their instructions. She would serve as the flight director, which put her in charge of the entire operation. She was the boss, which the twins understood.

Howard was in charge of the Trench—the team that worked out flight dynamics, guidance and retrofire to bring the astronauts back to Earth. Lisa would handle EECOM, which meant the environmental, electrical, and communications systems on board the Apollo CSM.

"Everybody's got to be ready to hit the ground running Monday morning," Egg said.

Mark frowned. "Uh, hit the ground?"

"Bad way to say it—sorry," said Egg. "Everybody's got to be ready to support launch, the mission, and the splashdown, I mean. We have a lot to learn, plan, and practice in a very short period of time. Are we in agreement? Howard, you'll have to talk to Steve Peluso tonight."

"Roger Wilco." Howard saluted. "Over and out."

CHAPTER 22

The news was on Grandpa's TV that night as the twins helped set the table for dinner. With the Washington Monument in the background, a politician was being interviewed on the steps of the Capitol building. The twins weren't paying much attention. They had a lot on their minds, plus they were hungry.

On TV, the politician, who was old, had silver hair, and a long face, said something that made the twins take notice:

"John Glenn is a bona fide American hero, but that doesn't mean he's right about everything. In fact, I have reason to believe that contrary to their assurances, the Salyut space station is armed with a powerful and potentially unstable warhead. This clear-cut violation of international agreements also makes it entirely possible that any rescue attempt might be met with calamity. I, for one, am not willing to put American lives at risk."

Scott was bringing in plates of food from the kitchen. "Who is that guy?" he asked his brother, who had crossed the room to look at the set.

Mark read the name printed at the bottom of the screen. "Senator Henry 'Scoop' Jackson, of Washington State."

Having come in from the kitchen, Grandpa pulled back his chair. "Turn off the tube, would you, please, Mark? I'm starved."

"Just a sec, Grandpa," Mark said. "I want to hear this, if it's okay."

Grandpa said, "Far be it from me to discourage your interest in current events."

The senator's voice continued: "Now, you fellas all know me, and I'm as sympathetic to the plight of a lone individual as any good American citizen. But we as a nation can't afford to let natural human sympathies interfere with clear-eyed defense policy."

The image changed to a baseball diamond, and the announcer said, "In other news . . ."

Mark turned off the set. Both boys sat down at the table. Grandpa didn't consider himself much of a cook, but he had a few solid recipes, including an awesome meat loaf. Scott covered his with a solid layer of ketchup from the glass bottle. It seemed to take several minutes to ooze out of its container.

It's too bad Earth isn't bigger, Scott thought. *Then there would be more gravity, and I wouldn't have to wait so long for ketchup.*

Meanwhile, Mark asked his grandfather what the senator on TV had been talking about.

"Ol' Scoop Jackson?" Grandpa took a sip of water. "He's what's known as a hawk—thinks the way to stay a step ahead of the Soviets is to spend a lot of money on defense, not to mention we shouldn't trust them farther than a man can spit."

"Is he right?" Mark asked.

Grandpa thought while he chewed and finally shrugged. "I'm no expert on international politics, but it seems to me it might improve our reputation around the world if we helped out that cosmonaut, whatever his political beliefs might be. As for whether it's risky, well, of course it's risky—warhead or no warhead."

The family ate in silence for a few moments, then Grandpa added, "One thing you got to take into account is this is an election year, and President Ford isn't very popular right now. The GOP is putting up Ronald Reagan to challenge him at the convention. And every Democrat you never heard of wants to run too—including Senator Jackson. These guys running for president are always saying things intended to get them on the nightly news and get them votes. Sometimes it doesn't matter if what they say is a bad idea."

Scott thought he understood. "So Senator Jackson only said that about a warhead to draw attention to his campaign?"

"Could be," Grandpa said.

Scott and Mark looked at each other. They sure hoped that was it. Otherwise, the rescue mission they were planning just might end with a bang . . . for real. And there was something else, too. If the Russians were the bad guys the senator said they were, was Barry at this moment flying into danger? What if the Russians thought Barry was some kind of spy?

After the dinner dishes were done, Scott and Mark cut a piece of string from the ball in the kitchen junk drawer and then went over to the shelf in the living room where Grandpa kept his globe.

"What are you doing there, Mark?" Grandpa asked. He was sitting in the big chair reading the paper as usual after dinner.

"Measuring," Mark said. "I was going to use the Atlas, but then I realized it's two-dimensional, so it doesn't take into account the curve of the Earth if, say, you happen to be flying over it."

"Are you still thinking about that poor cosmonaut?" Grandpa asked.

"I can't stop thinking about him," Mark said. "Can I borrow a pencil and paper, Grandpa?"

Grandpa nodded. "They're on the desk in my bedroom."

When Mark came back, he waved Scott over to the table, and the two of them sat down.

"What are you up to, anyway?" Scott asked his brother in a low voice.

"Trying to figure out where Barry is about now," Mark said. "If he left McGuire at eight, and the jet's flying six hundred miles per hour, he should be over Nova Scotia—that's in Canada."

Neither boy wanted to say anything to the other, but they were both worried about their friend. Was he going to be okay? What if he couldn't phone them when he got there? How would they know for sure he was all right? How would they know the Soviets hadn't put him in jail because they thought he was a spy or something?

Maybe they'd take him to the KGB headquarters, interrogate him, and ship him to a prison in Siberia. In that case, they would never see their friend again, and boy, would his parents be mad.

The twins really hoped that Senator Glenn's friends at the Russian Federal Space Agency came through. If they didn't, then Project Rescue might be over before it even got started.

Scott and Mark both wished they had thought all this over before Barry left, but there hadn't been any time for that then. Now it seemed as if they had plenty of time—plenty of time to worry.

CHAPTER 23

"I can't sleep," Mark announced a few minutes after lights-out. He and Scott were lying on their mattresses on the floor in Twin Territory, the loft where they always slept at Grandpa Joe's.

Scott did not reply.

"Can you sleep?" Mark asked. "Scott?"

Scott started awake and snorted. "What . . . did you say something?"

"It's important," Mark said. "I have an idea."

Scott's reply to this was regular, deep breathing.

"Scott? Sheesh—how can you sleep at a time like this?" Mark asked.

Scott rolled over to look at his brother's shadow against the window. "You could too," Scott said, "if you'd just stop talking."

Mark pushed his covers away. "We have to call the *Washington Post*," he announced.

Scott didn't answer immediately. He was thinking. *In a little more than twenty-four hours at this time,* he thought, *the window silhouetting my brother will be in the hull of a spacecraft, and the view outside will be either the stars of deep space or planet Earth itself.* In Scott's mind, this was exactly why he needed to sleep now. He was going to be pretty busy as soon as the sun rose.

But Scott also knew Mark would not let him rest until the big idea had been explained. "Fine," Scott said. "Why?"

"I'm worried about the Russians," Mark said. "I'm worried about their space weapon. Aren't you?"

"Sure," Scott said, "along with about five thousand other things."

"Well, this is one thing we can fix," Mark said. "Remember how it was *Washington Post* reporters who revealed the illegal stuff President Nixon's campaign did, the whole Watergate scandal? Eventually, the president himself was forced to resign."

Scott yawned. "I remember, Mark."

"So, let's say a reporter at the *Washington Post* gets a tip and writes a front-page article that tells the whole world two American kids are risking their lives to save a cosmonaut," Mark said. "If that happens, the Russians will have to do everything they can to keep us safe, see?

Otherwise, they would be embarrassed in front of the whole world! Also, it wouldn't exactly help Russian relations with the U.S.A."

"That whole détente thing Mom told us about," said Scott.

Mark nodded.

"But the reporter will try to stop us," Scott said.

"So we'll call when it's too late, like during the final countdown," Mark said.

"We'll be kind of busy then," Scott pointed out. "And besides, there's no telephone in the spacecraft, only the radio link to Mission Control."

Mark sat up. "Okay, so we work that out later. Right now, we should be writing down what we want the article to say. That'll make it easy for the reporter."

"Do you know what time it is?" Scott asked.

Mark didn't answer. Instead, he reached for his duffel bag and unzipped it. "I've got writing paper and a pen in here somewhere. You do the writing. Your handwriting is better."

In spite of Scott's reluctance, the twins were soon hard at work, writing as if the article would be appearing in the newspaper after the launch had already happened.

To convince the reporter and his (or her) readers that they were serious—and not just kids with crazy ideas—they included some real science in what they wrote.

To make the reporter's job easier, they tried to make what they wrote sound as much like a newspaper article as they could. Mr. Hackess assigned them current events every week, so they were used to reading newspaper articles.

WEST MILFORD, NJ—A team of kids from New Jersey is going to launch a mission to rescue stranded Soviet cosmonaut Ilya Ilyushin today.

If readers are wondering how kids are going to do this, please keep reading.

The kids were upset and shocked when both NASA and the Russian Space Agency decided to leave Major Ilyushin stuck in orbit. The kids believe that exploring space is a super-important scientific project for the whole human race, and people like Major Ilyushin—people who are risking their lives—should be supported by the whole human race, too. It doesn't matter what country the space explorers are from, or what kind of government the country has.

Because of some very amazing good luck, these kids from New Jersey have the equipment and the skill to carry out a space rescue. If readers are wondering how kids are going to do it, please keep reading.

The team is using a Titan launch vehicle borrowed from NASA to launch an Apollo spacecraft. The crew of the spacecraft is Mark and Scott Kelly, both twelve years old, both from West Orange, both twins. They blasted off from a new space facility near Greenwood Lake on the New Jersey and New York border.

Mission Control functions are being done by the ground crew, Jenny O'Malley, Howard Chin, Lisa Perez, and Steven Peluso. Another New Jersey kid, Barry Leibovitz, is assisting from somewhere near Moscow in the Union of Soviet Socialist Republics, also known as the U.S.S.R., also known as the Soviet Union, also known as Russia.

Scientifically, the most difficult part of the space mission will be the rendezvous with the Soviet space station, Salyut. That is where Major Ilyushin is stuck, with his air supply running out fast. There are probably animals stuck with him too.

A couple of things make a space rendezvous hard. One is that the thing you are trying to meet up with is traveling around Earth at a speed of nearly eighteen thousand miles per hour. Also, your spacecraft is traveling at a similar speed.

Another thing that makes a space rendezvous hard is orbital mechanics, which means the way objects orbiting around other objects behave. An object stays in orbit because the effect of gravity on it is balanced by its mass and its speed, in other words its momentum. The laws of orbital mechanics say that objects like spacecraft in lower orbit around a planet move faster than objects in higher orbit. This is because the gravitational acceleration, commonly called a g-force, is greater the closer you are to the planet.

If you want your spacecraft to catch up with a target spacecraft like Salyut, you start off in a lower orbit than the target so you'll go faster than it does. Then, when the ground radar tells your spacecraft that it is lined up with the target, you fire your thrusters forward, which accelerates you, pushing you into a higher orbit, and then because of orbital mechanics you slow back down. If your timing and math are perfect, it's the same orbit as the target, so now you are keeping pace with it a short distance away.

After that you can spacewalk over to the Russian space station to rescue Ilya Ilyushin.

Readers might be interested to know that a lot of the tools used in a rendezvous are actually pretty old-fashioned. For example, there is the sextant, which measures the angle between particular stars and the horizon to tell you exactly where you are in space. The sextant was invented in the eighteenth century, but even before that ocean navigators like Columbus used tools called astrolabes that work basically the same.

Another old tool is a gyroscope, a wheel spinning on its axis inside a frame called a gimbal. The gyroscope's spin creates angular momentum that keeps the wheel stable. The stable gyroscope can be used to measure the movement of what's around it. In other words, if the spacecraft spins, twists, or rocks, the gyroscope can tell how much.

The Apollo spacecraft has three gyroscopes mounted at right angles to one another in a metal box called an IMU, or inertial measurement unit. When they are all spinning at top speed, the gyroscopes keep the IMU in a fixed position.

The gyroscope was invented in the 1800s. Boats and ships use them too.

Finally, there is radar, which stands for radio detection and ranging. How it works is an antenna sends radio waves that bounce off whatever is in their way, like a Russian space station, for example. If you know how to read the bounced-off waves, you can tell where the space station is, how big it is, and if it is moving.

The idea for radar is almost one hundred years old, but the modern kind was invented just in time for World War II.

Scott glanced out the window of Twin Territory. He was glad to see it was still dark. What they had written so far was pretty good, plus there must be still at least a little time to sleep.

"What else should we add?" he asked his brother.

There was no answer.

"Mark?"

Still no answer.

If his brother was asleep, it looked like they were done with their article, whether it was ready for print or not. Carefully, Scott folded the paper in three and addressed it to: *Any Reporter/*Washington Post *Newspaper.*

Monday after breakfast, he would put it on top of Grandpa's stack of paper napkins, where Grandpa would see it at lunchtime. By then, he and Mark would be in orbit. With any luck, Grandpa would put two and two together and call the *Washington Post* and read it to somebody there.

Scott lay down and pulled up the covers. As he drifted off, he had a thought. Maybe by the time their article appeared in the newspaper, the ending would have been written: The successful splashdown of *Crazy 9,* and the rescue of Ilya Ilyushin.

CHAPTER 24

They had one more day to prepare for launch. The next morning, Sunday, at nine a.m., the team assembled at Greenwood Mission Control. Taking charge, Egg announced that the first thing to do was determine launch time, and the second was to establish the insertion burn to enable a circularized orbit.

Howard took a seat at one of the computer consoles and nodded. "Okay, I'll get moving on those."

Mark looked at his brother, who shrugged, and then he looked at Egg. "Uh . . . there's no such thing as a bad question, right?"

"Did I say that? I never said that," said Egg.

"It's Mr. Hackess who said that," Scott reminded him.

Mark fidgeted. "Okay. Well, never mind, then."

Egg crossed her arms over her chest. "Look. If there's something you don't understand, ask and I'll explain. That is, if I can explain. It's not like I know everything."

In their heads, Scott and Mark said the same thing at the same time: *You just act like you do.* But in real life, each one managed to keep his mouth from forming those words. Instead, Scott said, "Could you maybe remind us a little bit about that whole, uh . . . circularized orbit thing?"

Egg said, "Sure. And that's a good question."

Mark started to protest. "Didn't you just say—"

But Egg wasn't paying attention anymore. "You know a parabola is a rounded symmetrical shape, right?" she said. "Except it's not a circle because the points on it are not all the same distance from the center."

"Right," said Scott.

"Sure," said Mark.

"So *Crazy 9*'s orbit is a parabola," Egg said. "And its apogee, which is the high point, is roughly halfway around Earth from launch, while its perigee, the low point of orbit, is over a place very near the launch site."

"Right," said Scott.

"Sure," said Mark.

"So, for the rendezvous with the Salyut to take place, we have to change *Crazy 9*'s orbit from a parabola to a circle. You do that the same way you make any kind of adjustment to the spacecraft's flight path: you fire the rocket engines. What Howard is doing now is figuring out exactly when to fire and for how long."

As far as the twins could tell, Howard was completely absorbed in the green glow from his computer screen. But some part of him must have been listening, because he looked up. "Besides that," he said, "I have to calculate the rendezvous burn to catch up to the Salyut. And I could use some help with that."

"Okay," said Egg. "I can do that before I get going on the flight plan."

Mark nodded. "Hey, so cool. It's impressive the way you guys manage to keep busy. As for Scott and me, an astronaut's best preparation for spaceflight is recreation and relaxation. Scott?" He looked at his brother. "You want to take Grandpa's boat out or something?"

No one heard Scott's answer. Egg was yelling too loudly. Finally, Scott managed to raise his voice above hers: "My brother was kidding!"

Mark raised his eyebrows. "No, I—" he started to say, but Lisa interrupted.

"You guys need to get to know your spacecraft," she said.

"We already do," Mark said.

"We read this magazine article," Scott said.

"Yeah—and it had diagrams," Mark added.

Lisa shut her eyes and shook her head. Both Scott and Mark were surprised how much her expression looked like one of their mom's at that moment. "Unh-unh," she said. Then she opened her eyes and took a deep breath as if it was possible to inhale patience. "Follow me," she said.

This time the twins actually were joking. In the long months after Project Blastoff, they had done plenty of research on the space program. They knew, for example, that before the NASA people launched anything, they prepared for months and sometimes years. Engineers ran tests on every piece of equipment. They simulated everything anyone could think of that could possibly go wrong so they'd be ready. Anytime something didn't work right, it was fixed or redesigned and then tested again.

Besides the engineers, the astronauts practiced for hours and ran their own tests and simulations, sometimes backed by the Mission Control team and sometimes on their own.

In spite of all this, things sometimes went wrong. It was unavoidable. A spacecraft is built of so many parts that 99.9 percent perfection still means hundreds of problems.

NASA controllers had their own word for a mysterious problem. They called it a "funny." Some funnies did no real harm. Some could be identified and fixed right away.

But others were not funny at all, as both NASA and the Soviet space agency had learned from hard experience. On an American two-astronaut mission called *Gemini 6*, the Titan rocket engines stopped suddenly after ignition but before liftoff. The problem, identified much later, turned out to be a plug that jiggled loose. When the loss of the electrical circuit told the engine something was wrong, it shut down.

On a later Gemini mission, a short circuit made a thruster fire continuously, causing the spacecraft to spin so fast that the two astronauts onboard, Neil Armstrong and David Scott, almost blacked out. Had they done so, they could not have regained control of the spacecraft, and they probably would have died.

On a moon launch in 1970, with the bad-luck name of *Apollo 13*, faulty insulation on an electrical wire triggered an explosion that did so much damage it almost left the three astronauts stranded in space.

Small by themselves, each of those funnies had huge and nearly catastrophic consequences. And each one required an army of ground controllers, equipment designers, and engineers working tirelessly to keep the astronauts safe.

Mark and Scott didn't have a small army. They had Egg, Lisa, Howard, Barry, and starting tomorrow—Steve Peluso. They also had each other.

With Lisa, the boys ascended in the clackety-clack elevator and crossed the gangway to the spacecraft. Then the three of them pulled open the heavy hatch and took a look.

The Apollo command module was shaped like a bell, eleven feet tall, and thirteen feet wide at the base. The hull was made of steel and aluminum. To fit three astronauts, the gray interior was a lot bigger than the one-astronaut Mercury-size capsule in which Scott had flown before.

Still, it was pretty darned small, the size of a passenger car. And it was crammed full of complex electronics, including navigation and guidance systems, and radar to assist with the rendezvous. There were five windows, numbered one to five, left to right. There was one window each to the left and right of the outside seats, and one each in front of those two seats. The fifth window was a circular porthole in the hatch above the middle seat.

Scott climbed in first, grabbing the bar inside the hatch and swinging his legs inside, then crawling in a less than graceful way across the middle seat to the one on the left. Mark followed, taking the seat on the right.

It required a couple of grunts and shoves before they had positioned themselves, their heads on the narrow rest behind and their legs up above. Tomorrow, when they were outfitted in their flight suits, their boots would be locked into clamps.

This was not the most comfortable either of them had ever been, but comfort wasn't what they were thinking about. They were thinking about the main instrument panel above their faces. On it was a constellation of switches, gauges, and displays—including 50 different warning lights, 800 crew controls and displays, and 300 telemetry measurements.

On the walls to Mark's left and Scott's right were still more instruments. Mark's job would also include navigating, and his tools, a sextant and a telescope, were in the navigator's seat in the lower equipment bay. It was tucked under the middle seat, the one currently unoccupied but available for any stray cosmonauts the boys might encounter in their travels. Also underneath the seats lay a crawl space with lockers for food and equipment.

The boys knew all this "above" and "below" stuff would be meaningless once they were in flight, but while they were on Earth it was hard not to think of the layout in up-and-down terms.

"What do we have to do now?" Mark asked Lisa, who had remained outside to talk to them through the open hatch.

"You need to check over all of the spacecraft's critical systems—electrical, environmental, and reaction control," she said. "I'm going to head back to the Mission

Control building now. I'll communicate with you over the radio and monitor the operation remotely."

"She means she's gonna spy on us, bro," said Scott.

"I mean I am going to *help* you," said Lisa. "You guys will need to be looking for up or down arrows next to parameters on the panel. The arrows indicate if any of the metrics are out of desirable limits, either on the high or the low side."

"What do we do if we see one of those arrows?" Mark asked.

"We'll go to the checklist," said Lisa. "With any luck, it will have the procedure we need to address the problem."

Sitting in an unnatural position in the tiny crew compartment of the spacecraft, Scott anticipated the day ahead. It was going to be tough. It was going to require hard work and concentration. This flight would be different from *Crazy 8*'s, the one he had taken in the fall. In comparison to the machine he now sat in, that one had been a tin can. All it did was go up and around the planet and come back down.

But this spacecraft was the real thing. It was safer, for sure, but also a lot more complicated, and that would make it more difficult to understand and to operate.

Today's investment of time wasn't going to be fun. Unlike spaceflight, it would totally lack thrills and excitement. Still, it was necessary to the success of Project Rescue.

And something else was going to be necessary too. Lisa was right. They were going to need luck.

CHAPTER 25

Traditionally, astronauts eat eggs, steak, and orange juice before a mission. But the next morning—launch day—Scott and Mark couldn't ask their grandpa for such a fancy breakfast without making him suspicious. So, not knowing exactly when they would eat again, they each ate two bowls of Cap'n Crunch cereal instead.

How long were they going to be gone? That would be determined by the information Howard got from Barry. Once Barry gave him the precise location of the Salyut, Howard could calculate when to launch in order to rendezvous quickly and with the minimum amount of fuel.

Gulping the last of his milk, Mark thought of something else. Would Lisa remember to pack snacks? If she forgot, it could be a long, hungry day.

Lisa's dad's Cadillac was expected right after breakfast, but that wasn't the car that came up the driveway.

Washing cereal bowls, Grandpa looked out the kitchen window. "Who is that driving, can you see?" he asked Scott, who was putting away the silverware.

Scott grinned when he saw who it was. "Mr. Drizzle!"

A minute later, the twins were blasting out the front door. Mr. Drizzle was their friend but also the science teacher at Egg, Howard, and Lisa's school. His superpowerful solid rocket fuel, based on a unique composition of hydrocarbons chemically similar to sugar, had powered *Crazy 8* so successfully that NASA had reengineered the Titan rocket at Greenwood Lake to run on Drizzle fuel too.

Mr. Drizzle's car was a beat-up twenty-year-old Ford Fairlane that, apparently, had once been blue. He emerged stiffly from the driver's seat, stretched to his full height, and smiled. Mr. Drizzle had the flyaway pale hair and got-dressed-in-the-dark appearance associated with a mad scientist, but he was also friendly and good at explaining complicated things. Sometimes his explanations lasted longer than Mark, for one, would have liked.

Howard, Egg, and Lisa climbed out of the backseat. From the passenger seat came Steve Peluso. He was stocky, with wavy brown hair, small intense eyes, and pale skin apparently untouched by sunshine.

The twins' reunion with Mr. Drizzle was enthusiastic and warm. With Steve Peluso, it was courteous. Even if he was Egg's archrival, he was necessary for the good of the project. Scott and Mark both wished Barry were here. Barry was good at getting along with new and, uh . . . unusual people.

"My dad was too busy to drive us, and Mr. Drizzle happened to be picking up his car," Lisa explained.

"It's in the shop a lot," said Mr. Drizzle.

"I know whereof you speak," said Grandpa, and right away the two of them started one of those endless, boring adult discussions—this one about what it was like to own an old, broken-down vehicle.

Meanwhile the kids huddled and tried to bring Steve up to speed. "I know it's a lot to take in at once," Scott said.

Steve's expression said two things. First, he was thoroughly confused. Second, he didn't want to admit he was thoroughly confused.

"If my dad finds out I am helping you guys, he is going to have a cow," Steve said. "He doesn't like the Soviet Union. And he doesn't like people who disobey rules, either. He won't find out, will he?"

Lisa looked at Steve sympathetically. "It's tough to hide the launch of a rocket," she said. "For one thing, it's noisy. If you're afraid of your dad, maybe you'd better quit now."

For a millisecond, Steve looked so anxious that Scott thought he might cry. Then his expression changed. "I'm not afraid of my dad," he said firmly. "This is important and I'm going to do it. I feel for that guy in space. He's alone, and I know what that's like. Somebody has to help him."

"That's great," Mark said. "Egg and Howard will tell you what to do."

"But first," Egg said, "I have some other news. While we were driving here, Mr. Drizzle said it was a darn shame NASA wasn't using the spacecraft here at Greenwood to rescue the cosmonaut. Then after that, you know how it is, we kind of all got to talking about it, and, uh . . . well, one of us kind of mentioned maybe *we* were planning to rescue Ilya Ilyushin."

Scott's face fell. "You didn't."

"I never said it was *me* who mentioned it," Egg said.

"Well, was it?" Mark asked.

Egg tossed her straight brown hair. "I don't see that it matters, because what I'm trying to tell you is Mr. Drizzle says he'll help. He said it's the right thing to do, not only for the cosmonaut but to promote world peace."

Mark frowned. "Is Mr. Drizzle some kind of hippie?"

"He can help us," Egg said.

"I can use him to pinpoint the Salyut's orbit and help with rendezvous targeting," Howard said.

"Uh, excuse me. May I ask a question?" Steve asked. "How are we going to do that? Without the coordinates from the Soviet space agency, that is."

Egg answered. "Barry is going to give that to you. You remember Barry Leibovitz, right?"

"I remember him." Steve looked around. "Does he have a friend in the Russian space agency? Where is he, anyway?"

The jarring sound of the telephone interrupted. By this time, Grandpa and Mr. Drizzle had begun poking around under the hood of Grandpa's truck. "Excuse me," Grandpa said to Mr. Drizzle. "I better get that. Be right back."

A few moments later he called through the window, "Mark? Scott? Can one of you—"

The twins crashed into each other in their hurry to get through the front door. It was Tommy calling—had to be!

But when Grandpa held out the receiver, he said, "Ask him if he's taking good care of my coat."

Did that mean it was Barry on the line?

Scott grabbed, but Mark was quicker. "Hello? Mark Kelly here. Who is this?"

For a second, Mark heard no sound at all, then there was a hiss and finally a voice, faint but recognizable. "Hi. They won't let me talk long, but I'm okay, and . . ."

Scott, leaning his head against his brother's, couldn't hear what Barry said after that, but Mark listened intently. Finally, there was a crack and a click and then even the static went silent.

"Hello? Hello?" Mark shook the receiver as if that would fix anything.

"I think he's gone," Scott said, and the next sound was a dial tone.

"What's going on?" Grandpa was standing in the kitchen doorway. "Did I hear that right? Barry's in Russia? He sure sounded far away."

Mark shook his head emphatically. "No. Unh-unh. Not Russia. Not exactly Russia. He's in, uh . . . I think Secaucus. Secaucus, New Jersey. That and U.S.S.R.— they kind of sound the same."

"No, they don't," Scott said.

Mark looked at his brother. "*Sure they do.* All those Ss. Also, the Caucasus Mountains. Aren't they in Russia? Caucasus—Secaucus? I can see how you misunderstood, Grandpa."

"Mountains?" Grandpa scratched his bald head. "I never said anything about—"

"Anyway . . ." Mark shoved his brother past Grandpa, into the living room, and toward the front door. "It's cold in Secaucus, so Barry's real grateful to have your coat."

Outside, Scott whispered, "Shouldn't we have waited to see if he calls back?"

"No time," Mark said.

"You must've heard him better than I did. What did he say?"

"The Russian technicians are going to help him patch through to the phone line in our Mission Control center," Mark said. "As soon as he can, he'll talk to Howard, give him and Steve and Mr. Drizzle the information they need to compute the trajectories for the rendezvous."

Scott tried to picture his friend Barry, a kid he'd known since nursery school, on the ground with a bunch of Russian people at a secret military base called Star City. Apparently, he had managed to get there from the airport. Apparently, he had talked them into providing the help they would need—or maybe John Glenn's influence had done that.

Scott had flown into space only a few months before, but Barry's situation seemed even crazier and more perilous. What had he and his brother gotten their friend into, anyway? Some people believed the Russians were sworn enemies of Americans. Would they treat Barry okay?

Then he thought of something. The phone calls must be extreme long-distance. How much did they cost?

"Did he say anything else?" Scott asked.

"Yeah, one other thing, but I'm not sure I believe it," Mark said.

"What?"

"He said the goat cheese in Switzerland tasted pretty good."

CHAPTER 26

On the way down the dirt road to the launch facility, Mr. Drizzle's old car was stuffed with kids and their pent-up excitement. Even so, it was Mr. Drizzle himself who kept up a steady stream of conversation.

"I'm sorry," he apologized when he realized no one else was talking. "I'm just so excited!"

"We all are," said Lisa.

It looked like clowns at the circus when the kids piled out of the old car and headed for the Mission Control blockhouse. Almost the instant Egg switched on the lights, the phone rang.

Howard got to it first. "Barry?" he said hopefully, then he smiled one of his rare smiles. "Man, am I glad to hear from you. Steve!" He waved. "Pick up a phone and press the button that's lit, see? Mr. Drizzle, can you pick up too?"

Steve and Mr. Drizzle did as they'd been directed and began to listen intently. Mr. Drizzle pulled a slide rule off his belt and started penciling calculations on graph paper. Howard pressed a button on a computer keyboard to bring it to life, then began entering data.

A whole lot of variables go into setting a course for a spacecraft and keeping it there. Where the thrusters are pointing, how much fuel is being burned, how much mass is in the fuel and the spacecraft, the gravitational pull of Earth, the moon, and the sun—all these affect the navigation. Meanwhile, the team also had to predict how much fuel each and every maneuver was likely to use to ensure that the spacecraft didn't run out.

While Howard and his team talked to Barry, Egg turned to Scott and Mark. "Where's your flight plan?" she asked.

Mark nodded agreeably. "Flight plan. Right," he said.

Egg rolled her eyes. "What were you doing last night, anyway? Didn't you finish up the flight plan?"

"We ate a good healthy dinner to nourish our growing bodies," Mark said. "Does that count?"

"No," said Egg. "But fortunately I've got my own draft of the flight plan right here." She handed over a clear plastic folder. Inside were many pages of lined notebook paper covered in neat handwriting.

"Did anybody ever tell you that you have lead-er-ship po-ten-tial?" Scott asked her.

Egg was too busy to respond. She turned to Lisa. "Lisa, you have the prelaunch schedule, don't you?"

"Right here," said Lisa, and she read aloud. "Breakfast, thirty minutes. We can check that one off. Then ten minutes for a physical, ten minutes to put on the pressure suit, twenty-five minutes to test the pressure, and five minutes to walk over to the launch tower and ride up to the white room."

Egg looked at her watch. "Okay, ten minutes for the physical."

"How do you guys feel?" Lisa asked the twins.

"Physically or mentally?" Scott asked.

"Both," said Lisa.

"Mentally, the only thing that worries me is being cooped up in a small space with this guy," Scott said.

Mark nodded. "Back at you, bro."

"Okay, in that case I declare you sane," Lisa said. "How about physically?"

"I'm not sure I should've eaten that second bowl of Cap'n Crunch," Mark said. "Otherwise, fine."

"Same here," said Scott.

"You'd better get going, then," said Egg.

"Yeah, you'd better." Howard by this time was off the phone. He looked a little pale.

"What is it?" Scott asked. "Is Barry all right?"

"Yes," Howard said. "At least he didn't say he wasn't. We were kind of too busy to ask."

Then Howard looked at the clock on the Mission Control wall and drew in a deep breath. "We have to start the countdown *now* at T-minus-60 minutes," he said. "Given the Salyut's current orbit, our best rendezvous time will be 1400 Zulu or MET 05:30:00. That's midway through orbit three, or about five and a half hours into the mission. If we don't make that, the next-best rendezvous point is five days from now—"

"Five days!" Scott repeated. "But we can't—"

"We can't, and neither can he," said Howard. "By then Major Ilyushin won't have good atmosphere anymore."

Unlike Howard, Egg did not look rattled. She tapped her pencil against her clipboard and spoke up. "Okay, everyone, take your places, pull out your checklists, and get to work. Howard, you need to specify the added velocity for each maneuver.

"Mr. Drizzle? You'll be updating the delta V as the flight goes forward to calculate the de-orbit burn for reentry. We're looking at a daytime landing, I hope? Tomorrow morning?"

Mr. Drizzle looked as happy as a kid at a carnival. "Roger!" he said.

"Lisa? You're done being flight surgeon. Now you're going out with the twins to precheck the cabin and set up the switches."

"Roger," Lisa said.

Scott couldn't wait to get going. Having been in space

before made him eager to go back, and gave him confidence that everything would turn out okay. Mark was eager too, but if he was honest with himself, he knew he also felt scared.

On the short staircase to the exit, he looked back at Egg, Howard, Steve, and Mr. Drizzle, all hard at work, and felt a tug that was sort of like affection. Also, he wished he had said a better good-bye to his grandfather that morning.

Scott looked back impatiently at his brother, but when he saw the expression on Mark's face, he understood. "Come on," he said, his voice deeper than usual. "We gotta go. We gotta get this done."

CHAPTER 27

Without much discussion, the boys decided in the elevator that Scott would fly as commander and Mark as pilot. It made sense, since Scott had been in space before. Ordinarily, the commander would do the EVA, leaving the pilot in charge of his ship. But since both boys desperately wanted to float around in space, Lisa offered to flip a coin.

They had emerged into the white room by this time. Lisa took out a quarter from her jeans pocket.

"Heads!" Mark called—and heads it was.

"Two out of three?" Scott said.

"Ha—you wish!" Mark said.

"Okay, fine," said Scott. "Just don't expect me to wait around if you're late getting back."

Inside the white room, the astronauts suited up as

efficiently as possible with Lisa's help. Once in their suits, they turned on their oxygen supply. Breathing oxygen for a while before launch would get rid of the nitrogen in their bodies. Otherwise, when the cabin was depressurized for the space walk, that nitrogen would form bubbles in their bloodstream—a painful, dangerous condition known as "the bends."

With their tight countdown schedule, the boys were barely buckled into their seats when Lisa leaned in one last time and secured shoulder harnesses, seat belts, oxygen hoses, restraining clamps, and communications wires.

"Kelly twins to the rescue!" she said, and gave them a thumbs-up.

Scott looked up from his checklist to say thanks, but she had already lowered the hatch. Mark, who was closest, unstowed the locking handle and cranked it shut.

Meanwhile, Mark and Scott went to work, checking switches, making sure electrical circuits and pipes supplying water and oxygen were all in good working order, turning off unnecessary circuits.

They cycled the computer through its software programs, then checked the control system, the radio frequencies and telemetry, the tracking beacons and guidance system. They armed the pyrotechnics, took a look at the battery voltages, and pressurized the reaction control system. In spite of their preparation the day before, both twins felt like they were scrambling to keep up as the countdown progressed.

Mark was updating the altimeter when he felt a jolt. "What's that?" he asked his brother, alarmed.

Scott didn't even look up. "Access arm swinging away."

"Oh, sure, okay," Mark said. A moment later, there was another bump. "What was that?" he asked.

Scott grinned. "What a nervous Nellie," he said. "It's the rocket engines being gimbaled—swiveled around to make sure they move like they're supposed to. Don't worry. I'll tell you if it's something bad."

Lisa by this time was back at Mission Control, and her reassuring voice came on their radio headsets. "Wind is at sixteen knots. Scattered clouds at two thousand feet, visibility fifteen miles."

"We are T-minus-3 minutes and counting," said Egg. "*Crazy 9*, do you read?"

"Loud and clear—too loud. You don't have to yell," Scott replied.

The minutes ticked down. On the radio, Mark and Scott heard Egg poll Howard, Mr. Drizzle, and Lisa on the systems for which they were responsible.

"FIDO?"

"Go!"

"GUIDANCE?"

"Go!"

"EECOM?"

"Go!"

"*Crazy 9*. This is Greenwood Control. Are you go for launch, Scott?"

"Go!"

Egg summed it up: "All systems are go for launch at T-minus-2 minutes."

It wasn't totally silent in the CSM. Oxygen hissed in the pipes, and fans whirred. Mark and Scott could hear their own breath inside the helmets, which they would wear for launch and remove once they were safely in orbit. They didn't know it, but at about the same time each thought to himself: This is dangerous and crazy but totally cool!

At T-50 seconds, electrical power was transferred from the launchpad to the command module. At T-minus-9 seconds, the lights on the panel blinked as the first-stage engines of the Titan ignited, and thrust began to build. Mark watched the clock, the engine lights, and the tank pressure meter. He had never felt such a strange combination of joy and terror as he did while listening to Egg's calm voice:

"Five . . . four . . . three . . . two . . . one . . . liftoff!"

There was a low rumble followed by a solid surge of power—*Is this normal?* Mark wondered—and then, two seconds later, the twins felt a jolt as the big bolts that had been holding the rocket in place fired to release it. A moment later, the electrical umbilicals to the launch tower dropped away. Then, with 430,000 pounds of thrust behind it, the Apollo CSM rose from the pad. It was 10:30:99 ET, and *Crazy 9* was leaving New Jersey behind in the rearview mirror.

"Liftoff, and the clock is running," said Scott, then, ten seconds later, "clear the tower."

Before Mark's eyes, the instruments were going nuts— lights shone, dials jumped, the computer burped numbers. The spacecraft rose slowly at first, then, abruptly, the power in the fuel won its struggle with gravity and Mark and his brother hurtled skyward. With the noise and vibration, Mark couldn't help remembering that he and his twin were balanced on top of a missile.

He tried to steal a look at Scott's face, but couldn't.

If something felt wrong, Scott would know and say so, right? And if something were *really* wrong, he would twist the T-shaped handle by his left hand that aborted the mission and ejected them from the spacecraft.

"Pressure good, temperature good, azimuth good at seventy-five degrees," said Lisa.

"We are green and go," said Egg.

"Roger, Mission Control," Scott responded. "Just took a quick peek outside, and the view is incredible. This thing sure has better windows than *Crazy 8*."

By the time *Crazy 9*'s velocity reached Mach 1—the speed of sound—the control panel in front of Mark was shaking so much it was hard to read the gauges. The first-stage fuel tanks were emptying out now. Soon all the fuel would be gone and the first-stage engine would shut down and separate. At which point, the Titan's second stage would take over.

"Staging," Egg said. "One hundred thousand feet, two and one-half minutes."

The G-load had been near five—pressing the twins into their seats—but now it dropped back to one, same as on Earth, and then it kept right on falling till Mark's body rose within its harness, nearly weightless.

Mark's eyes had been intent on the instruments in front of him. Now he looked out the window and almost wished he hadn't.

It was hard not to keep staring out the window at the planet, but he still had work to do.

Now the g-forces mounted again. Eight minutes into the flight, they hit seven, and Mark felt like a giant gorilla was sitting on his chest. "It's just like the roller coaster at the Great Adventure amusement park," he reminded himself. "We'll be over the hump in a sec, and then I'll be able to breathe."

"One hundred miles now," said Egg. "Stand by for second-stage engine cutoff. Looking good, *Crazy 9*! Right down the alley!"

Another jerk, and the second stage rocket shut down, then—on schedule—it, too, detached from the CM and fell away.

Crazy 9's flight path started vertical, then arced southeast. By now, the boys were over the Atlantic Ocean at an altitude of one hundred miles and a speed of 17,500 miles per hour.

"Mission Control, *Crazy 9*, we are downrange two hundred miles," Scott said.

"Flight path looks good," said Egg.

At last, Mark felt free to relax for a minute and take in the view. Scott had tried his best to describe it to him after *Crazy 8*, but Mark saw now how inadequate the description had been. Sunlight streamed through the windows, but with no atmosphere to turn the sky blue, it remained dark outside. Earthward, the overwhelming impression was of brilliant color, distant blue ocean, brown-and-green coastline, every variety of cloud imaginable. Mark was filled with awe . . .

. . . and at the same time he felt something else filling his head, something uncomfortable. In response to weightlessness, his bodily fluids were rising into his head and face. *Ew!*

This was not a good feeling at all. Mark had read that astronauts' faces puffed up like chipmunks' in microgravity. Until their bodies adjusted, it was like hanging upside down on the jungle gym.

"Pretty, isn't it?" Scott said.

Mark snorted, trying to clear his sinuses. "Yeah, it's really something else."

Then all at once they both laughed. They were relieved

to have survived the launch. They were excited to be in orbit. And it was comical to use plain words to describe the magnificent spectacle of Earth below them.

The twins loosened their chest straps. They had checklist after checklist of things to accomplish if they were going to rendezvous on time. As he got to work, Mark noticed something else to worry about. Tiny pieces of the spaceship itself seemed to be floating everywhere—screws, bolts, washers, and blobs of cement compound.

Was *Crazy 9* disintegrating?

At the risk of sounding like an idiot, he asked his brother.

"No, no, don't worry about it," Scott said. "Anything that got dropped during construction reappears in weightlessness. In a little while it'll get sucked into the ventilation system and start to clear up. If we had had more time, we could have vacuumed before launch."

Bits of spacecraft weren't the only things floating around. Mark's hands floated too. It was a strange sensation to have to work to hold them down.

"*Crazy 9*, come in, *Crazy 9*," Egg said. "We'll be losing radio contact shortly."

"Roger, Mission Control," said Scott.

"But we have a UHF lock for you to communicate with Barry in Moscow when you're in range—about twenty-five minutes if all goes well, at MET 00:40:00, I mean. We'll upload the link from here. Stand by."

CHAPTER 28

According to the flight plan, the rendezvous would take place during *Orbit 3*. Periodically during the next few orbits, Howard at the computer at the Greenwood Lake Mission Control center would feed updates into the *Crazy 9* guidance system. Once the changes to their trajectory had been loaded into the computer on board the spacecraft, Mark and Scott would configure the propulsion system and perform a burn of the reaction control system engines to change their flight path. This would bring them closer to the Salyut.

Between rendezvous burns, Scott and Mark could sit back and enjoy the ride. Staring out the windows, they tried to figure out where they were over the planet. Sometimes it was obvious, like when they passed over the Mediterranean Sea and looked down on Spain and the boot of Italy, which looked, well, just like a boot.

Other times they had no idea what that was below them. Were they over Australia or the United States? It all looked the same.

What was obvious was that the planet below was big, round, and incredibly beautiful, and they were traveling around it at nearly 18,000 miles per hour. If you looked straight down, you could tell you were going that fast. Five miles of land or water passed beneath them every second.

Mark switched his radio to the intercom loop so he could talk to his brother without everybody else listening in. "I thought Earth would look smaller," he said, "like it does in those photos from the Apollo missions. Instead it's huge! It fills the whole window."

"The moon missions traveled almost two hundred and fifty thousand miles away from Earth. Compared to that, we're not very high up at all. While we are still above the atmosphere, we are only about two hundred miles above the planet's surface," Scott said.

"Is there any atmosphere up here?" Mark asked.

"A little bit," said Scott, "enough to create a small amount of drag. But altogether, Earth's atmosphere is scary thin. You can see that when you look at the horizon."

Mark did, and it looked to him as if the atmosphere was so fragile it would blow away in a cosmic storm.

Scott continued, "If Earth were an orange, the atmosphere wouldn't even be as thick as the peel."

"You sound like Mr. Drizzle," said Mark, then he straightened out his legs for a few seconds, trying to get comfortable. He couldn't. His back had started to hurt. He complained to his brother.

"Oh yeah, mine, too," Scott said. "It's normal, I think."

"It is?"

"Yeah, you know how your backbone is made up of little bones called vertebrae?" Scott said.

"Sure," said Mark.

"Well, without gravity, they spread apart, and the muscles around them have to stretch to make them fit. The stretch is what you're feeling. If we were in space long enough, you'd get used to it. You'd get taller, too," Scott said.

"I wouldn't mind being taller," Mark said.

"The uncool part is your bones get weaker," Scott said. "Bones need weight on them to stay strong. That's one of the reasons the Skylab astronauts in space for weeks had to work out every day. They were trying to fool their bones into thinking they were still on Earth."

Scott's lesson on bone density in space was interrupted by a crackle of static. Someone was trying to talk to them. It couldn't be their Mission Control. They were on the wrong side of the planet for radio signals to get through.

"*Crazy 9*? Come in, please. This is the Soviet Union Mission Control center in Moscow. *Crazy 9*, do you read?"

Barry!

And he sounded closer than he had on the telephone. Well, the truth was that he *was* closer—only about two hundred miles straight down, thousands of miles less than the earthbound distance from New Jersey to Moscow.

Mark and Scott both wanted to ask how he was, what the U.S.S.R. was like, if the Soviets were being nice to him. But all that would have to wait. Now they had to stick to business.

"Moscow, this is *Crazy 9*. We read you. Have you talked to Ilya Ilyushin? Is he expecting company?"

"Hi, Scott! Good to hear your voice. Uh, well, actually that's a negative on Major Ilyushin."

Scott's heart skipped a beat. If Barry hadn't talked to Major Ilyushin . . . did that mean they were too late?

Barry must have read his mind. "*Crazy 9*, don't panic. We have reason to think the cosmonaut is okay. The atmosphere in the Salyut should still be good. There doesn't appear to be any damage to the ship. Best we can figure it, the trouble is with communications. We are still working on it."

"Roger," said Scott. "Uh, so what do you want us to do?"

"We are go for rendezvous at approximately 06:30:00 hours MET," Barry said. "Worst case, you can knock on the door, and we hope he lets you in. We have a secret code for you to use when you knock. Mark, are you ready for instructions?"

A secret code? Mark thought. *How cool is that?* Even with its hard work and discomfort, this space rescue thing really was a blast. "Roger, Barry—that is, Moscow. Go ahead."

Totally prepared to commit a complex sequence to memory, Mark was surprised when Barry revealed it: "Long, short-short, long, long, rest, long, long."

Mark tapped his knee to try it out. "Hey, wait a sec. Isn't that shave-and-a-haircut, the old-fashioned rhythm Grandpa taught us?" he asked.

"Roger," said Barry. "I guess the Russians and Grandpa do have some stuff in common."

Scott had an anxious thought. "Barry, are you sure you're understanding everything they're telling you? No offense to your grandma, but your Russian isn't that good."

Barry laughed. "Roger that, but it gets me plenty of caviar. There's an interpreter here who was married to their top space guy, the one who died. Her English is really great, plus she knows a lot about science and engineering.

"We'll be losing radio contact soon," Barry went on. "Flight control here says as of now, the distance between *Crazy 9* and Salyut station is six hundred and forty miles. Do you read?"

"Roger," said Scott.

"Howard will be instructing your onboard navigation system to lift the apogee of your orbit to two hundred and twenty-two miles with perigee one hundred and forty-four miles."

Circling the globe roughly every ninety minutes, the twins went from day to night and back again until their bodies were thoroughly confused. How long had they been in space anyway?

They were once again over New Jersey, where it was late Monday afternoon, when Mr. Drizzle's voice came on the radio. "*Crazy 9*? I have you tracked on the ground radar. Looking good, but we're going to need a few adjustments. Oh my, but this is *so* much fun!"

Scott grinned. "Roger, Mr. Drizzle. Yeah, we're having fun too. Uh—what were those adjustments exactly?"

Up till now, Scott and Mark had allowed first the Titan launch vehicle and then the computer to do the flying. Now Scott, in the left-hand seat, had to demonstrate his own piloting skills. Protruding from the instrument panel was a T-shaped translational controller. A translation is a change in orbit; in other words, nearer to Earth or farther away.

On Scott's right armrest was the attitude controller, which was kind of like the stick on a jet or an airplane. Attitude is the vehicle's orientation in three-dimensional space. When Scott pushed the attitude controller, the nose of the spacecraft rotated down. When he pulled it, the nose came up. Push the controller right, it rolled right, and left made it roll left. Twisting the controller caused a left or a right flat turn, which is called a yaw.

With Mission Control watching their every move, Scott followed Mr. Drizzle's directions, and they began to close the gap on the Salyut, now 460 miles away.

It was nighttime again and *Crazy 9* was over the eastern Pacific when at last Mark spotted a tiny blinking light out the window. Of course, there were stars all around, but if this had been a star, it would have shone steadily. It's Earth's atmosphere that makes stars appear to blink. From Mark's current vantage point, they shone steadily.

That meant the blinking light could only be one thing, the Salyut space station.

CHAPTER 29

At this point they were close enough that Mark needed to take on a new responsibility: navigator. He unbuckled his harness, pretzeled himself in two, then alternately climbed, crawled, and dove down to the lower equipment bay, where the navigator's seat was located. On arrival, he enjoyed a brief, full-length stretch. This was the only place in the CSM where that was possible.

Then he went to work. His job was to help his brother, Commander Scott, zero in on *Crazy 9*'s location in relation to the Salyut. To do that, he peered through a sextant built into the hull of the ship. Using it, Mark scanned the sky till he located three stars, Schedar, Hamal, and Vega. Then he measured the angles between them and the horizon.

The stars' unmoving position in the universe is known to the computer. Using trigonometry, it found the spacecraft's position in relation to them, and then compared it to what it knew about the rendezvous target, the Salyut station.

The computer display read 000.00. "Five balls!" Mark announced, the nickname the Apollo astronauts had given the display when they were perfectly on course.

Out the window, the Salyut grew from a blinking dot to a human-made satellite, one that was a whole lot bigger than the CSM. Now all Scott had to do was avoid crashing into it, which would not only be fatal, it would be embarrassing.

To prevent that, he got constant updates from Egg on the distance to the target, also known as "range," and the speed at which they were closing in on it, the "range rate." When both reached zero, the rendezvous had been accomplished—hopefully without any crashing involved.

As Scott used his controllers to keep *Crazy 9*'s nose pointed at the Salyut, Mark continually measured the rate at which the CSM's angle above the horizon changed. When the computer told him the moment was right, he told Scott to translate to the Salyut's orbit, and the altitude difference between the two ships began to shrink.

As *Crazy 9* closed to within a couple of miles, the Salyut changed from a flashing light to a shiny blob to a sixty-foot-long cylinder with two sets of twin solar panels like insect wings. Inside, the boys knew, were three compartments for cosmonauts and one for the engines and control equipment.

While the Apollo CSM had been built for basic transportation only, the Salyut was effectively a very fancy mobile home, and its three interior compartments were plenty big enough for standing up (if there was an up) and moving around.

"Coming up on one minute," Scott reported to Greenwood, "chamber pressure is holding, gimbals good, attitude good, rates are damped out."

"Roger, *Crazy 9*," said Egg. "Steady as she goes."

Mark felt his heart racing. He and Scott had studied the Apollo program and the spacecraft itself. They both knew plenty about how the CSM was supposed to fly and how a rendezvous was supposed to work. But this was the moment of truth.

Mark peered through the sextant again, this time using it and a clock to measure how fast the Salyut appeared to be growing, which gave him a rough measure of the rate at which they were closing in on it.

"Range 250, rate 50," Mark said, meaning they were 250 feet away and were moving at 50 feet per second—only 5 seconds to *crunch*. "Slow it down a little, bro." He tried to keep his voice calm.

"Roger." Scott fired the forward-facing thruster jets, braking the CSM.

"Range one hundred and fifty, rate thirty," Mark said—still five seconds. "Better."

Scott waited for a count of three. Now they were sixty feet away, then fifty, then forty, then thirty. . . . The Salyut loomed huge in the windows, blocking out the sky.

"Uh . . . what are you waiting for, bro?"

Scott's answer was to fire the forward-facing thrusters again. The braking effect was not as fast as Mark would have liked, and he closed his eyes, expecting any second to hear a horrible crunch of metal on metal.

There was no Nando's repair shop in space, no tow trucks either. If Scott had miscalculated, they had just made things a whole lot worse for the stranded cosmonaut—not to mention the pickle they were in themselves.

But there was no crash.

Mark opened his eyes.

Crazy 9 was parked about ten feet away from the Salyut hatch. The red Soviet flag with the yellow hammer and sickle was plainly visible on the side, as was the closed hatch. Without realizing it, Mark had been holding his breath. Now he breathed.

"Sheesh," he said to his brother. "You cut it a little close, didn't you?"

Scott was grinning. "I didn't want you to have to walk too far."

CHAPTER 30

Essentially, *Crazy 9* was now a taxi from the USA parked outside a big Soviet mobile home. As they reached the Pacific, the sun appeared once again over the horizon. They would be back in radio contact with Greenwood Control shortly. With luck, Barry would have called in by now to say that communications were back, and Ilya Ilyushin was expecting them.

But before that, Scott had something he wanted to say.

Capped by his success in maneuvering the CSM to its position beside the Salyut, this day had been the most emotion-packed of any he could remember—more emotional even than when he had gone into orbit on his own. Now, watching his brother work, he felt his chest tighten.

Just go ahead and say it, he decided. *No preliminaries.*

"Look, bro," he said at last, "uh . . . I won't leave you out here."

Mark wasn't really listening. He was pulling out the AMU, the astronaut maneuvering unit, which would serve as a jetpack for his EVA. "I'm glad to hear that," he said, then something about Scott's tone made him add, "Wait, what do you mean?"

"I mean," Scott said, "if anything happens, if you get stranded like Major Ilyushin is, if there's some kind of malfunction, if you can't get back . . . You know that's possible, right? The EVA is the most dangerous part of the mission."

Mark felt uncomfortable. Not scared. By this point a certain amount of scared seemed normal. What made him uncomfortable was this kind of talk, especially from his brother. "I know it's dangerous," he said cautiously.

"Okay, then," said Scott. "So here's the thing. I am not leaving you. I am not going home—I am not facing Mom and Dad—without you."

Mark didn't hesitate. "Oh yes, you are. If I can't get back, there's no point in you, uh . . . not getting back too. It'll be up to you to tell Mom and Dad and Grandpa and everybody, uh . . . to tell them . . . that they're really great, and I was thinking of 'em. Okay? Is that a deal? You have to carry the message. And you have to promise, too."

This was not the way Scott had wanted the conversation to go, but now he saw his brother was right. "Okay," he said reluctantly. "I promise. I guess. And now you'd better get ready to EVA to the rescue, or there was no point in either of us coming up here in the first place."

From the storage bay beside the AMU, Mark retrieved a white nylon zippered disk with a diameter of around forty-eight inches. He had identified this piece of equipment only the day before, when he and his brother were getting to know their Apollo spacecraft. At first, it was a mystery to him, but testing it, he found it reminded him of the pop-up dome tent his family sometimes used for camping.

Naturally, it had been Egg who explained.

"It's a personal rescue ball," she said. "At least, I think it must be. As far as I know, NASA has never actually used one yet, but they must have had prototypes manufactured. It makes sense, I guess. One of the reasons they stationed the spacecraft at Greenwood Lake was for rescue purposes."

"Okay," Mark had said, "but what is it?"

"The idea is an adult curls up in a ball and climbs in," Egg said "Then you pressurize it and the oxygen keeps him alive during the space rescue. I'm not sure for how long." She had recommended he take it with him to the Salyut.

"It's not like it's heavy, right?" she said.

"Well, it won't be in space," Mark said, "because out there nothing's heavy. But Ilya Ilyushin has a space suit, doesn't he?"

"We don't know what kind of shape he'll be in, or it, either," said Egg. "The rescue ball might be useful as a backup."

Even though only Mark was going to leave the cozy confines of the spaceship to venture into space, both boys would be putting on their space suits. These were the ones they had tried on in the white room, different from the flight suits they wore for launch and reentry in that they were fully pressurized and carried their own oxygen supply. In preparation for Mark's departure, Scott would vent the atmosphere in the CSM till the interior pressure was zero—same as in the near vacuum of space.

After that, they would open the hatch. On Earth, it was so heavy it took at least two people to do this. In space, once the latches had been released, the hatch rose with the tiniest pressure.

Putting on space suits, venting the oxygen, and opening the hatch—it all sounded quick and easy. But it took almost two hours to accomplish. The fifty-step checklist, developed by NASA, had to be followed exactly. A missed hose connection, a buckle left unbuckled, a glove improperly attached—any of these things would cause catastrophe.

The boys understood this and, as goofy as they could be on Earth, they took the process seriously. Both of them planned on having futures, even if that did mean they would have to grow up.

"You'd think weightlessness would make things easier, wouldn't you?" Scott asked as—for what seemed like the hundredth time—he went looking for his copy of the flight plan Egg had given them.

"It's more like the opposite, isn't it?" Mark agreed. "When there's no down, you can't exactly set something down. And every time I do, it just floats away."

"Yeah, in theory stuff would just stay put," Scott said. "But with the air currents from the fans, stuff gets pushed all over the place. Have you seen my flight plan?"

Mark was having troubles of his own. Securing a strap, he had let go of a pencil, and now it was gone. "You should keep better track of your stuff," he answered irritably.

"What are you? Turning into Mom?" Scott wanted to know.

When at last they were suited up, Mark announced, "I don't think getting dressed for school is ever going to bother me again."

Scott agreed, "Yeah, it's funny how you don't appreciate little things, like gravity and atmosphere, till you have to live without them."

"On the other hand, look at this!" Mark said. In the lower equipment bay, there was just space to do a somersault. Now he tucked himself into a ball and set himself spinning . . . and spinning . . . and spinning. It was fun for the first few fast rotations, and then he got dizzy. By the time he heard Egg's voice, he realized spinning had not been the best idea.

"*Crazy 9*, Greenwood Lake, do you read? *Crazy 9*, come in, please. Are you go for the EVA?"

Scott answered. "Roger, Greenwood. Uh, hi, Egg. We are all set. Have communications been reestablished? Is Major Ilyushin expecting company?"

"Well, not exactly," Egg said. "And the problem remains unidentified. In the best case, it's just signal interference. You should know, though, that there may be some risk we're not aware of."

"We read you, Greenwood, and yes, we're go. We haven't come this far just to wave off." Scott was confident he was speaking for his brother, and—even though spinning had made him feel a little nauseated—Mark gave a thumbs-up to confirm.

CHAPTER 31

"*Crazy 9*, you are go for cabin de-press."

"Roger, Greenwood. We read you. Venting the cabin now."

The designers and engineers who built the Apollo spacecraft did not want it leaking oxygen everywhere, so the depressurization procedure was tricky and, like everything else, required a checklist. Item by item, Scott and Mark went through it, flipping switches, twisting controls, and watching regulator displays.

As the air was released from the cabin, the pressure in their suits made them balloon and stiffen. Scott remembered what Lisa had said about turning into a snowman. There was definitely some truth to this.

Greenwood Mission Control ran a last check on all systems, then Egg sent up official permission for Scott to open the hatch. Scott reached for the big handle over his head. He was about to ask his brother if he was ready, when Mark spoke up. "Uh, wait a sec," he said. "Remind me again how we know everything in here, including you, isn't about to get sucked into space?"

Scott couldn't believe his brother. "You are a knucklehead, you know that? The cabin's depressurized, right? So the pressure in here is the same as it is out there. It's like if you submerge a jar totally full of water in a bucket full of water and open the jar—the water in the jar doesn't get sucked out. The pressure's the same both places."

"Or a jar full of air in a bucket full of air," Mark said.

"You got it," said Scott.

Mark nodded. "Okay, okay. Just double-checking. You can go ahead now."

Again, Scott reached up. Again, Mark said, "No—wait. One more thing."

Scott sighed. "Okay, what? You know we don't have forever, right? We'll be back in darkness in forty-five minutes, and we'd like to get this done while it's still light."

"I just have one more question," Mark said. "While I'm floating around outside, you, that is *Crazy 9*, you won't get ahead of me, right? I don't want to have to swim to catch up. *Crazy 9* is traveling faster than a bullet leaving a gun."

Scott was getting impatient. His brother understood

all this, didn't he? But then Scott figured something out: His brother was nervous!

Well, of course he was!

And it was the least Scott could do—as a good commander—to allay the fears of his crew, even if those fears made no sense.

"*Crazy 9* is traveling something like ten times faster than a bullet, but so are you," he said patiently. "And remember Mr. Newton"—he meant Isaac Newton, the great English scientist who lived in the seventeenth century—"and his three laws of motion."

Mark was confused. "You mean action–reaction?"

"No, not that one," Scott said. "The first one. An object in motion—you—stays in motion unless some external force interferes. Right now you're in motion, traveling at 18,000 miles per hour. You just don't feel it because we're all moving together and so is the Salyut. We might as well be standing in New Jersey and all rotating together on Earth's surface. Earth rotates at around 900 miles per hour, depending on your latitude, but you don't have to run forward to keep up with it, do you?"

"No," Mark said, "but how about after I leave the ship . . . ?"

"You are also an object in motion," said Scott. "So according to Mr. Newton, you're going to keep traveling at 18,000 miles per hour. Just don't crash into any external forces, like the Salyut space station."

The truth was that Mark's brain did know this, but it was a lot different to know it when you were sitting at a library table reading a physics book than when you were about to pop out of the hatch of a spacecraft.

"You feel okay, right?" Scott said. "You're not dizzy anymore?"

"Sure. Uh, kind of. Why?" Mark said.

"Because if you puke, it's not just a blinding mess in your helmet, it'll probably kill you." Scott's hand moved toward the unlatching mechanism on the hatch again.

"Wait a second," Mark said. "What do you mean?"

"The throw-up will clog your oxygen line. You'll suffocate," Scott said matter-of-factly. "Or you could drown in your own vomit. Are you ready to go now?"

Mark thought for a moment about all the things that were going to kill him in space. It was a long list. But of all of them, this would be absolutely the most embarrassing.

What would it say on his tombstone? "Here lies Mark Kelly, a brave astronaut, killed by his own vomit."

This, Mark decided, could not happen. So he swallowed hard. "I am fine," he said, and he willed his stomach to follow orders. "Okay, Commander Scott. Let's go. What are you waiting for, anyway?"

CHAPTER 32

"Greenwood Lake," Mark radioed to Earth. "I am now going for a walk."

The view through the window of *Crazy 9* had been the most awe-inspiring spectacle Mark Kelly ever saw or expected to see.

And it was nothing compared to the view when he floated out of the hatch.

He gasped.

He said, "Oh my gosh," which was stupid but also as good as any other words a person might use when confronted with the grandeur of the entire universe coming at him from every direction.

Astronaut Gene Cernan had told the press that spacewalking was like being inside a kaleidoscope, and that was the best description Mark could come up with himself. Everywhere he looked, the colors of the universe glowed and sparkled, shapeshifted and spun. For a dead and empty vacuum, space sure did seem alive.

Because Mark and *Crazy 9* were speeding onward at ten times the speed of a bullet—Mark remembered what Scott had said—the dawn came fast, changing the dark from gray to blue to gold till at last the sun appeared, white and fiery, to light Earth. Mark recognized the distinctive shape of Baja California jutting into the blue Pacific, then the golden desert sand of the southwestern United States.

In contrast, the view of space beyond was now utterly black, the stars blanked out by the sun's illumination.

Mark knew that ten years before, when the first American astronauts had space-walked, psychiatrists had worried they might suffer from something called space delirium. The view might make them crazy, in other words. Mark was pretty sure he wasn't crazy. Instead, for the first time in his life, he really understood the meaning of the word "awe."

Outside, the view was beautiful . . . and, more than that, *strange*.

All the episodes of *Star Trek* and *Lost in Space*, all the TV pictures of NASA missions to the moon—none had prepared him. Was this really the same universe that also contained New Jersey, where Mark had awakened that morning, that contained his parents, his school, his friends?

He was grateful his brother was nearby in a spacecraft that seemed so solid.

Mark could have enjoyed the view for hours. An EVA really took the word sightseeing to new levels. But he had only about forty-five minutes to accomplish the rescue before night fell. In darkness, everything would be just that much harder.

The first spacewalkers had been connected to the spaceship by a cord containing electricity, oxygen, and communications wiring. In weightlessness, the cord became as unpredictable and dangerous as a writhing snake. So Mark would move around using only the AMU on his back. Scott had tethered the rescue ball to a D-ring on the back of his suit, and it trailed him like a round, awkward tail.

"Hey, Mark—what's it like?" Scott asked over the intercom.

"It's like . . . it's like . . . well, there's colors, bright colors, uh . . . and Earth looks like Grandpa's globe, only in the sun it's bright, lit up."

"Don't look at the sun!" Scott ordered.

"Aye aye, Commander."

"Hey, cool, but you've got work to do!"

"Yeah, okay. Uh . . . be right back."

The checklist for the AMU was twenty pages long. Mark had already understood the general idea, but he had had time for only a quick review before he'd strapped it to his back. If you cut through the details, the operation was straightforward. There were controllers by each hand that powered tiny nitrogen thrusters. You pushed the left control for forward and back, and twisted the right one for up and down, left and right.

The Salyut station was only a few feet away. He set out by pushing gently against the side of the Apollo CSM and—*whoosh!*—popped straight up at a terrifying rate. "Wait, that's not what I wanted"—he twisted the right controller to correct and suddenly was heading for his feet, and beyond them the Grand Canyon, which was in the opposite direction. If he wasn't careful, he was going to crash into his own spacecraft—*splat!*

After a few seconds, Mark realized that if he moved any part of him even a little, he would move the other way. With very little in the way of friction or gravity to complicate matters, Newton's third law of motion was fully in charge: Every action yields an equal and opposite reaction.

Clearly, he had to use a lighter touch. Scott had been watching him out the window. "Stop fooling around!" he ordered.

"I'm not!" Mark felt irritated with his brother, who couldn't possibly understand. He was safe in the cocoon of the ship. Something else irritated him too. Mark was breathing hard. It was an effort to fight the awkward oversize space suit, now pumped up to 3.7 pounds per square inch of pressure. The suit might not be made of silver metal like a suit of armor in the old days, but it was so stiff it made Mark think of what it must have been like to be a knight. Even bending an arm or a leg was hard work. And it was made for an adult, so he didn't exactly have the best fit.

At last, calling on patience and fine motor skills he didn't know he had, Mark managed to propel himself over to the hatch of the Salyut, arriving with only a gentle bump rather than the resounding *crash* he had feared. There was just one problem. The hatch had disappeared.

"Greenwood Lake, this is Spaceman Mark. Do you read? Egg, can you patch me through to Barry?"

"Moscow Control here, Spaceman," Barry replied. "Egg already did the patch. Are you inside yet? How's Major Ilyushin?"

"That's a negative, Barry. Uh . . . where's the door?"

"Try the shade side," Barry replied. "The primary crew module is set to rotate for passive thermal control."

The Soviet Union had helpfully placed handrails on the outside of its space station. Mark took full advantage of these, climbing hand over hand until he came to the hatch. Next to the handle for the unlatching mechanism was a label. Some of the print was red and boldface, a warning about something.

Mark hoped it didn't say AMERICAN ASTRONAUTS, KEEP OUT.

Using his fist, hardened by its all-protective space glove, Mark knocked on the hull of the space station, using the "secret code" Barry had given him. Now he was glad it wasn't some complicated sequence. With all that he had on his mind at this moment, he never would have remembered it.

If there was a response, Mark didn't hear it. The only sounds were the hiss of the oxygen in his suit and the crackle of the communications link. Anyway, in space there was no air to carry sound waves and therefore no sound. Inside, though, the metal hull of the ship would carry the vibration of his knocking so the cosmonaut could hear it.

That is, if the cosmonaut was alive to hear it.

Time passed. Mark realized he was holding his breath. What if he and his brother had come this far— if Barry had gone all the way to Moscow—and it was all for nothing? Any one of a million things could have gone wrong on the space station. Maybe it wasn't just a communications problem at all. Maybe it was something much worse.

CHAPTER 33

Third time's the charm, Mark thought, and he knocked out the secret code—shave-and-a-haircut—once more.

Again moments passed, and now Mark was worried about minutes ticking away. He had plenty of air to breathe. That wasn't the problem. Light was the problem. The rescue operation needed to be completed in daylight. It wouldn't be long now before he would have to return to *Crazy 9*—with or without the stranded cosmonaut. He hated to admit failure, but he was on the brink of doing so when he realized that the hairline crack between the hatch's edge and the space station had begun to widen.

Then, at last, with excruciating slowness, the hatch began to rise.

There was something disturbing about this that

Mark hadn't expected. He felt like he was watching the front door of a haunted house open slowly on Halloween night. He had a crazy urge to turn tail and power back to his brother and his own familiar *Crazy 9*.

Was Major Ilyushin even alive?

What if it was his ghost that was opening the hatch?

What if it was a scary space alien?

Mark took a deep breath and told himself to settle down. Maybe there wasn't enough air in this space suit after all. What else would account for these crazy thoughts?

I know very well there's no such thing as ghosts, he reminded himself. *And as for space aliens, maybe there are some on some planet somewhere, but why would they show up right here right now?*

The only reasonable explanation for the hatch opening was that Major Ilyushin, a human just like himself, was opening it.

The only reasonable explanation, he repeated to himself. *The only reasonable explanation.*

Within a few seconds, the opening between the hull of the ship and the hatch widened enough for Mark to slip inside. Using the handholds, he bent at the waist, positioned his feet, then, and with much trouble and many contortions, he push-pulled himself from brilliant reflected sunlight into gloomy darkness.

"Hello?" he said, knowing this was a waste of breath. He had his helmet on, and even if Major Ilyushin had been right there in front of him he couldn't have heard. Still, it would have been too weird to enter someone's house without calling a greeting.

"Greenwood Control, this is Spaceman; come in, please. Can you patch through to Moscow to tell Major Ilyushin I'm here? Do the communications work yet?"

"I'll try, Spaceman," said Egg. "Are you inside? Is he okay? And how are the animals? What's it like there?"

"Sheesh, Egg—how should I know what it's like? I can't even see anything. I can't even move."

"Sorry," said Egg in a small voice.

Mark guessed he had to be in the airlock module, tight quarters, and he couldn't move his bulky suit backed with the AMU without bumping into something.

"Spaceman," Egg said, "Moscow says the crank for the hatch is behind and above you. If you reach up, you'll find it. After it's closed, Major Ilyushin can re-press the airlock."

"Wait, so Major Ilyushin knows I'm here?" Mark asked.

"I can't get a straight answer at this time," said Egg. "But either way, you've got to close the airlock."

"Roger that." Mark found the crank and turned it. The hatch came down slowly. He wasn't claustrophobic, but this was ridiculous. He was now in a tight space (his suit) within a tight space (the airlock) within another tight space (the Russian space station). Every fiber of his being had developed itches that he could not possibly scratch. Besides that, he could barely see.

"Okay, I've got it," he said. "Now could you ask pretty please if Major Ilyushin could let me out of—*aaaaaaaaiiii!*"

"Spaceman? *Spaceman?* Do you read?" Egg's voice was no longer small, it was loud and frantic. "Come in, Spaceman? Oh, Mark, oh *no*—are you okay?"

Scott's voice was next up. "Mark? Come in, Mark Kelly! Look, I take back all the bad things I ever said, only *please*—"

Scott's radio transmission was interrupted by a loud *thonk*. Then there was a *crackle* of static followed by the all-too-human sound of someone breathing hard and fast.

"Mark?" Egg repeated, her voice an anxious whisper.

"I'm okay, I'm okay." Mark sounded breathless.

"What happened?" Egg asked.

"The interior hatch opened all of a sudden, and the light practically blinded me. The power's on, that's for sure, and—*aaaaaaaii!*" Mark squealed again, but this time he recovered more quickly. "Uh, hi? Hello? You must be Major Ilyushin. Am I right?"

CHAPTER 34

The brilliant light caused Mark's vision to blur for a few moments. When at last the view came into focus, he realized first that he was in the crew compartment of the Salyut, second that a man was suspended in front of him, and third that the expression on the man's face was such a wild-eyed combination of surprise and terror that it would have been comical in other circumstances.

As it was, Mark figured his own expression was probably about the same.

As quickly as he could, Mark undid the fastenings and removed his helmet.

"Ilya?" he said . . . stupidly, because who else could it be?

A little of the terror left Major Ilyushin's face, but

none of the surprise. "You are American?" he said, eyeing the American flag on the sleeve of the space suit. "You are a small boy?"

This was not the greeting Mark had looked forward to. "I am not small," he said. Then he held out his hand and said politely, "It is a pleasure to meet you, Ilya."

The cosmonaut took Mark's hand but raised his caterpillar-fat black eyebrows. "You may call me Major Ilyushin. In the United States, it is also correct for a child to use the honorific when he addresses an adult. Is that not true?"

Mark didn't know the word "honorific," but he got the idea. "Sure. Major Ilyushin. Sorry. You can feel free to call me Mark, though. I've, uh . . . heard a lot about you."

Most conversations in the Apollo command module took place when you were strapped into a seat. There wasn't space for hanging around. But here in the Salyut, there was. Now, both he and Major Ilyushin were suspended weightless in the middle of the comparatively large compartment. It was strange and awkward trying to hold a conversation with someone who was floating, and Mark grabbed a handgrip on the ceiling—or was it the floor?—to prevent his unintentionally drifting one way or the other.

"In contrast, I have not heard about you," said the cosmonaut. "Here in the space station are electrical anomalies that have affected communications with

Moscow. Do they know about you in Moscow? How is it that you are here?"

Mark flashed back to playing "Save the Dog" with Major Nelson on the living room rug. Major Ilyushin didn't seem to want rescue any more than Nelson had.

"I guess I can see why you're surprised," Mark said. Since this wasn't a good time to discuss politics or Scoop Jackson or NASA, he explained as best he could. "I was the only one available, I guess, that is, my brother and me and the crew at Greenwood Lake. See, we don't have school. It's Easter vacation in New Jersey."

Major Ilyushin's reply was a curt nod.

"Uh, is there Easter vacation in the Soviet Union?" Mark tried to make conversation.

"*Nyet*," said Major Ilyushin.

"Right," Mark said. He was sorry he wasn't getting a more friendly reception, but he decided to give the stranded cosmonaut a break. After all, Ilya Ilyushin had been in space by himself for weeks, besides which he had probably expected to die.

Anybody would be grouchy.

"So, Major," Mark asked courteously, "what seems to be the trouble?"

Before Major Ilyushin could answer, Mark heard something unexpected—a bark. Was there a dog on board? Till now, he had forgotten about the animals reported in the news.

Major Ilyushin scowled and moved to the far side of the module where a set of three plastic boxes was suspended for brackets. They looked like pet carriers. "*Tishe*, Richard Nixon! *Tishe!*" Major Ilyushin snapped.

Richard Nixon? What does the former president have to do with anything? Mark wondered.

"Shall I let him out?" Major Ilyushin asked. "I suspect he will enjoy an opportunity to meet with a new and unfamiliar person."

Wait a second.

Was Richard Nixon a *dog*?

Mark knew a lot of people in the United States considered the disgraced president to be a criminal, but Mark had never thought of him as a dog before. "Uh, so why did you name him Richard Nixon?"

Major Ilyushin shrugged. "Russian humor. It is hard to explain." He raised the wire door at the end of the box. Out of it shot a blur of spotted energy whose pink tongue sent perfect spheres of dog slobber caroming everywhere.

The dog was small and sturdy with a short, spotted coat and floppy ears. Mark was impressed with how comfortable he seemed in weightlessness, just like Major Ilyushin himself. Soon he was licking Mark's nose and spinning as if he wanted his belly scratched. Mark tried to oblige, unintentionally sending the dog ping-ponging in the other direction.

This didn't seem to bother Richard Nixon any. He just pushed off the floor—or maybe it was the ceiling—and tumbled back for more.

"There are rodents as well," Major Ilyushin said. "Mice and cavies—what do you call them in the U.S.A.?"

"Cavities? What?" Mark was confused, but then he heard another animal noise, this one a combination burble, squeak, and chirp. "Oh! Guinea pigs!" He remembered the sound from his second-grade classroom. "So that's what you've got in the other two pet carriers."

"*Pet?* No, no, *nyet* pet!" said Major Ilyushin. "These animals are for only experimental purposes."

Mark remembered what his dad had said: germ warfare! But, somersaulting around the space station, Richard Nixon looked plenty healthy. And anyway, there was no time to worry about germs or warfare, either. He and Major Ilyushin had to get down to business. Daylight was fast running out.

Moscow and Greenwood were in agreement. It would be best for Major Ilyushin to go home in the Russian transport ship, the Soyuz, if that was possible. So the first thing to do was isolate the problem with the Salyut station and then, if possible, fix it.

Of course, the *Crazy 9* team knew a whole bunch of Soviet scientists and engineers had already tried to do this, but their previous success had given them confidence. It was a funny thing, but sometimes inexperience enabled you to see something everybody else had missed. It was worth a try.

Now Major Ilyushin explained the problem: "The Soyuz spacecraft in which I came to the space station is now hard-docked to it. The first step in the undocking procedure is to release the main docking latches. To do so, I throw this switch." He indicated a silver tab on an elongated black instrument panel similar to the ones in *Crazy 9*. Beside it, a red warning light glowed. Major Ilyushin moved the switch back and forth. No matter what he did, the red light continued to glow. "You see? The switch does nothing."

"How about this?" Mark said. "Can you release the latches manually?"

Major Ilyushin frowned, causing his two eyebrows to become one. "If I could do that, would I still be here?"

Mark nodded. "Yeah, good point."

"I believe," Major Ilyushin continued, "that one of the electrical circuits has, what do you say in English— shorted out? The engineers on the ground have told me that even if we could locate the problem precisely, the only way to make a repair would be to slice the metal skin of the space station. This is impossible without a blowtorch, which I could not use anyway for obvious reasons."

Mark knew what those reasons were, too. In the pressurized environment of the space station, the spark from a blow torch would cause an explosive fire.

Mark said, "Let me talk to our engineers about it," and by "engineers," he meant Lisa. "She, that is, *they*, might have an idea."

Major Ilyushin sighed and shook his head. "And are these engineers also children?"

Mark said, "Some people might call her, that is, *them*, children. But they're supersmart children, smarter than me even."

Major Ilyushin looked doubtful, and Mark thought maybe after all Egg would have made a better astronaut. She would be better at the meeting-new-people and promoting-world-peace part. He switched on the transmitter in his helmet, which he had left suspended conveniently beside his head. "Greenwood, this is Spaceman, come in, please."

Once the situation had been explained, Lisa was quick with a reply. "Is there an auxiliary power switch for the signal conditioning equipment—the SCE?"

Major Ilyushin could hear Lisa's amplified voice. "Ask her what she is talking about," he said.

"I heard him," Lisa said, "and I don't know how to say it in Russian. We could patch through to Barry's interpreter, but that would take a while. I'm talking about the equipment that provides backup voltage to instrumentation points in the control and fuel cell systems. Can he, that is, can *you*, switch it to aux—to auxiliary?"

"Ah," Major Ilyushin nodded. "I now understand, and I know the system to which you refer, Engineer Lisa, but the Soviet engineers, in their surpassing wisdom, have built no redundancy into this system."

There was another pause before Lisa replied. Mark thought she must have been thinking. Was she out of ideas? "Okay, roger," she said at last, "so then here's another idea. Give the instrument panel a solid whack with your fist."

Major Ilyushin's eyebrows did an unhappy dance, and Mark could tell the cosmonaut's opinion of Lisa had fallen to a new low. "Is she—what is the word? Kidding around?" he asked.

"I heard *that*, too," Lisa said, "and no, I am dead serious. On the *Apollo Fourteen LM*, the lunar module, a stray piece of wire got into a switch and bounced around, interrupting the circuit intermittently.

"Of course, they didn't know that till later, they just knew that sometimes the signals the switch sent were all wrong. They almost had to abort the mission. Then one of the controllers had the smart idea of thwacking the panel by the switch—problem solved. Apparently the thwack dislodged the stray piece of wire."

Mark didn't follow Lisa's whole explanation, but he got the point. He should ball up his fist and hit the panel beside the switch. And, without waiting for Major Ilyushin's permission, that is exactly what he did. Nothing happened for about a second, then, like magic, the red light turned first amber, then green, and a moment later, from deep inside the space station, came a *thump*, then the sound of a metal mechanism humming to life.

"Lisa, you're a genius!" Mark said, and—for the first time since Mark had removed his helmet—Major Ilyushin smiled. "I am going home!" he said.

But his joy did not last long.

When a moment later the cosmonaut turned his full attention to the instrument panel, he saw that a new red light was illuminated . . . and his face went pale.

"Mark Kelly," he said in a strained voice, "you and I—we are in imminent danger, *mortal* danger! There is no time to prepare the Soyuz or even to explain. Put on your helmet. We will leave immediately through the airlock."

What the heck?

Mark didn't know what Major Ilyushin had seen on the panel, what that new red light meant, but the look on his face and the way he spoke made it obvious he was scared to death.

Mark grabbed his helmet and prepared to abandon ship. At the same time, Richard Nixon tugged at the fingers of his glove. He was just like Nelson, Mark thought. He wanted to play!

Major Ilyushin saw Mark's face and must have read his thoughts. "We cannot afford to be sentimental about animals. We must save ourselves."

Mark took a deep breath. He was all in favor of saving himself. But then he looked into Richard Nixon's trusting brown eyes . . . and he couldn't leave him behind. And if he was going to grab the dog, well, he might as well take the guinea pigs and mice, too.

"You go," Mark said. "*Crazy 9* is stationed right outside. Big American flag on the hull, you can't miss it. My brother—that is, Commander Kelly—he knows you're on your way. Tell him I'll be over in a sec."

CHAPTER 35

One thing soon became obvious about the rescue ball. It was designed for slow-motion rescue, *lazy* rescue—for all those times you were in no hurry with your rescue— certainly not for those times when a terrible, painful, and unknown thing was about to happen any second.

Released from its zippered nylon case, the rescue ball popped open and expanded, becoming a sphere twice the size of a beach ball. It would be a tight fit for a human astronaut, but for one small dog, four mice, and three guinea pigs, it was plenty big.

The setup was ridiculously complicated—Tab A, Tab B, twist this and tighten, push this probe into that latch until it clicked. Repeat.

It seemed to take forever, but at last Mark had the oxygen tubing hooked up and the power on, and the sphere itself looked the way he hoped it was supposed to. Inside, there would be room for only a single pet carrier. The guinea pigs and the mice would have to share, but at least it wouldn't be for long. The flight plan called for splashdown less than three hours from now.

"You guys are okay together for a few minutes," Mark said to the rodents. "No fighting." Then, with the lightest possible touch, he pushed Richard Nixon in after. The dog didn't mind a bit; in fact, he wagged his tail. Like any good astronaut or cosmonaut, he was always up for a small space or a new experience.

Mark looked around the Salyut station once before closing the hatch on the airlock. The station looked ordinary. It was large, well lit, and comparatively welcoming. What could be so dangerous, anyway? Could it really be that bad? Maybe Major Ilyushin was exaggerating.

Earth had spun once more into darkness by the time Mark exited into space, twisted the left-hand control on the AMU, and began the short trip to his own command module. The universe, previously a kaleidoscope, was now every shade of shadow, with his own Milky Way galaxy arcing around him like luminous smoke.

Below, Earth was a dull and lifeless gray. Since the moon was not up, the only earthward light came from occasional lightning flashes in the storm clouds. Venus, in contrast, was lit like a lantern.

After a while, Mark thought, a person would get used

to moving around in space just like you get used to being in the water. Both Richard Nixon and Major Ilyushin, he had noticed, were a lot less awkward than he was.

But would you ever get used to this view? It would be sad if you did, if this spectacle became routine rather than overwhelming and distracting. And speaking of distracting—*bump, buh-bump*—he had run into the hull of the command module with more force than he had intended—*ouch*.

"Commander Kelly, come in, bro? Spaceman, here. I'm back."

Once Mark was inside, he was eager to tell his brother all about his adventure, but for some reason Scott did not want to hear it. "Strap in and stow the animals," he said.

"But—" Mark began.

Major Ilyushin, who had taken his place on the middle seat, interrupted. "There is no time for warm reuniting between brothers."

"*Move it, Mark!*" Scott commanded, then, "Greenwood Lake? *Crazy 9*. We are getting out of here."

Because there is no atmosphere either to fuel a fire or to carry a sound, explosions in space don't last long, and they don't make noise. So when a few minutes later the Salyut space station blew up, the explosion consisted of a single multihued and brilliant flash.

"Don't look!" Scott said, and Mark closed his eyes,

but even through his lids, he felt painful pure white light. The lack of sound felt like a silent scream, all the more frightening because it was so strange. An instant later, a cloud of whizzing, broken, dangerous debris rat-a-tatted against the hull of *Crazy 9*.

"Brace positions!" Scott shouted. "Stay clear of the windows!"

Tense moments passed before Mark stole a look out the window. The debris swarm by now was moving harmlessly into the endless beyond.

Had it been true? All that talk about the Soviet Union and space weapons? Had the Salyut been armed with bombs, nuclear bombs? Had he and his brother been exposed to deadly radiation in exchange for saving the cosmonaut's life?

When Mark could breathe again, he asked, "Wh-wh-what happened?" His heart was going a mile a minute. If the rescue ball had been any more complicated, if Richard Nixon had hesitated to go inside, if he had admired the view any longer—the blast would have been deadly.

As it was, Scott and the flight control computer by now had maneuvered the command module to a lower orbit, and *Crazy 9* was in one piece.

"I guess it's a good thing I hurried," he said weakly. Then, when neither Major Ilyushin nor Commander

Kelly replied, he went on, "Uh . . . so what happened? What did you see on the control panel, Major I?"

The "Major I" had just slipped out. It was so much easier to say than Major Ilyushin. Mark expected the cosmonaut to scold him for being disrespectful, but he didn't. Instead, he explained.

"It would seem that your entrance into the Salyut space station caused pressurization to drop below the threshold set by the automatic environmental system," he said. "To compensate, the system pumped oxygen into the crew compartment—too much oxygen. Had I been monitoring continuously the panel, I would have seen that this was happening, and I could have vented some of the oxygen into space. But by the time I realized there was a problem, it was too late for that.

Major I did not have to explain the risk further. In an overoxygenated atmosphere, the tiniest spark would cause a fire. Such fires in highly pressurized enclosed spaces had killed three American astronauts in 1967 and a cosmonaut in 1961. Only quick thinking and good luck had prevented a third such fire on the Soviet mission that included the first space walk in 1967.

Since the Salyut space station's electrical system had been working unreliably, the likelihood of a spark was high.

Sky-high.

The best explanation for what had just happened

was that an oxygen-rich fire had ignited the remaining
fuel on the Salyut Space Station . . . and caused it to
explode. During the *Crazy 8* mission, and this one too,
the grown-ups had warned over and over, "Please don't
blow anything up." Now it looked as if they had—and it
wasn't even their fault.

One thing about a space walk, it really makes you hungry.

Luckily, Lisa had remembered the snacks.

To avoid the dangers of crumbs interfering with
equipment, Lisa had made them NASA-style and packed
them in plastic sandwich bags.

"Uh, what is this stuff?" Scott asked after sucking
a sample through a drinking straw carefully inserted
through a corner of the bag. They were somewhere over
Africa, out of Greenwood Mission Control radio range,
so there was no way to consult the chef.

"I don't know and I don't care, I'm starving." Mark
sucked a taste through his own straw and announced,
"Peanut butter and jelly sandwich, I think. All ground up
and mixed with water. Tastes great to me. What do you
think, Major I?"

"Jelly I know, but not peanut butter. It is NOT good.
We Russians do not eat peanut butter. I prefer borscht.
Do you have borscht?"

"*Nyet* borscht," said Mark, thinking Barry would be
proud of him for speaking Russian. "Sorry."

Fortified by food, Mark worked up the courage to ask their guest whether there had been weapons on board the space station.

"*Nyet* weapon." Major I was so emphatic that both boys believed him. "You Americans are paranoid," he added.

"What about germ warfare?" Mark asked. "Is that what the mice and guinea pigs are testing?"

"No, no, not that," Major I said. "It is a simpler test to see about the long-term effects of life in space for biologic entities. You see, each one has a littermate back on Earth whose health has been monitored while he was in space. Now our Soviet scientists are going to compare one to the other to find out about the effects of space on their bodies."

"Hey, we're littermates too—Scott and I, I mean," said Mark. "Maybe someday NASA could do that with us."

Scott nodded. "Maybe," he said, "provided anybody at NASA is still speaking to us after we get back. We kind of stole their rocket."

CHAPTER 36

Scott had already experienced the thrill ride of de-orbit and reentry on the *Crazy 8* mission in the fall. The second time through, he enjoyed it more—even the part where *Crazy 9* became the center of an ionic fireball, and all radio communications were blacked out. The only problem had occurred shortly after the de-orbit burn, when pummeling by the atmosphere caused the pet carrier containing the rodents to pop open, and all of a sudden guinea pigs and mice were bouncing and flying everywhere.

Richard Nixon watched the flying rodent circus with interest, but he was too good a cosmonaut to bark. Fearing he might see his little buddies as potential doggie treats, Mark and Scott were glad he was safely strapped in. Meanwhile, Major I watched unhappily as Earth's gravitational force kicked in and a guinea pig descended slowly into his lap.

As they hurtled back to Earth like a big rock, Mark thought to himself again about the risk involved in going into space. They were nearly at the end of their mission, but still so many things needed to go right and in correct order and at the right time.

Once the big red-and-white parachutes had deployed, Mark breathed a sigh of relief and relaxed. "This little guy over here is having a great time." He indicated a mouse with its paws planted firmly on the control panel. It seemed to be studying the artificial horizon.

"I think he's preparing for his next flight," Scott said.

"And he expects a promotion to mousetronaut," said Mark.

Of all the beautiful sights Mark and Scott Kelly had seen during their long day, the last one was the most beautiful of all: Grandpa rowing out to meet them as they floated in the command module in the middle of Greenwood Lake.

Naturally, Mr. McAvoy was relieved and overjoyed by his grandsons' safe return. At the same time, he couldn't help adding, "Don't you ever do that again! My heart can't take it a third time."

"It is a pleasure for me to meet you, Mr. McAvoy," Major Ilyushin said with great formality as he settled himself into the boat. "Your grandsons were very brave and surprisingly intelligent and skillful. Tell me, are all American children like this?"

"Well, of course, I think the twins here are pretty special," said Grandpa, "but then, I'm biased."

As Grandpa began to row, Major I looked at his surroundings curiously. "Previously to now," he said, "I had always thought that returning American astronauts were met in a great ocean by helicopters and aircraft carriers."

Grandpa nodded. "That's one way they do it," he said, "but we here at Greenwood Lake are kind of a low-rent operation."

While they had awaited Grandpa's arrival, Scott and Mark had rounded up the rodents and returned them to their carrier. Now the carrier was in the keel of the boat, and the guinea pigs could be heard chittering happily.

From the back of the boat, Richard Nixon looked toward land like a scout. Major I said his legs felt a little shaky after their weeks in weightlessness, but Richard Nixon was wagging his tail, happy to be back amid earthly smells and gravity.

"Now, none of you needs to talk to the press right yet," Grandpa advised them. "Jenny's mom—Mrs. O'Malley—has kept them at bay so far. It might be best if you let the NASA press relations people handle that part, at least for the time being."

"Did the *Washington Post* run our story?" Mark asked.

"You bet they did. Front page this morning," said Grandpa.

"And did Steve Peluso get in trouble with his dad?" Scott asked.

Mark looked at his brother curiously. The last person on Earth he, Mark, was thinking of at this moment was Steve Peluso. But then, his brother was often a mystery to him.

Grandpa laughed. "I think Steve and his dad the school board member have worked things out. You'll understand more about how that happened when you get to shore."

Crazy 9 had splashed down twenty-one hours after launch. It was now seven thirty in the morning on Tuesday. The twins were tired and hungry. Lisa's snacks had been nutritious, and even tasty if you didn't think too hard about how you were eating liquefied peanut butter and jelly, but they were not very filling for two growing boys. Major I was still craving borscht.

Onshore waited almost every human being who mattered to Scott and Mark—their parents, the Greenwood Mission Control team with *their* parents, Barry's mom and dad, and Tommy. Behind friends and family were emergency personnel, with the red lights on their vehicles flashing, and then members of the press, waiting with pens and microphones poised. Flashbulbs popped sporadically, klieg lights shone like stars.

It was a lot to take in—especially given how hungry and sleepy the boys were—but they had expected it. There had been a crowd for Scott's return on *Crazy 8* as well, but nothing like this.

There was, however, one person waiting whom the boys couldn't place. They had spotted him from a distance, a fit-looking man dressed informally in khakis and a white shirt. As they got closer, they noted his thinning, sandy hair. There was something special about him. His square shoulders. His perfect posture. The way other people made a space for him.

Scott stared for a few more oar strokes, then gasped. "Grandpa, that's not—?"

Grandpa looked back over his shoulder and nodded. "John Glenn. I forgot to mention. Nice fellow, too, if a little correct in his speech. I guess that goes along with being an American hero."

When at last they got to shore, it was Senator Glenn who greeted them first, then reached in a hand to help Major Ilyushin. "Feeling a little wobbly, I expect, after so much time in zero-G?" The senator smiled. "Welcome back. And welcome home to you, young men. That was quite a stunt you pulled."

Stunt? Mark and Scott looked at one another. Wasn't it true that the senator was on their side?

"Yes, sir, Mr. Senator Glenn, sir," Mark said as he climbed out of the boat. "I mean, no, sir. I mean, stunt, sir?"

"These children were very brave," Major I said, "and very competent fliers as well. I have not till now met, I think, such, what do you call them here in America? Such 'kids'? Or is this the word for baby goats?"

"You can call us kids if you want," Mark said.

"It's better than children, actually," Scott added.

"Ah. I must work on my English," Major I said. "However, what I want to say at this moment, I am able to say. I am very very grateful to my rescuers. And for the future, if you want to call me Ilya, that would be acceptable."

The senator smiled. "These young men did a brave thing all right, and it was a nice piece of flying as well. Of course, they had help from a solid team on the ground." He gestured to Egg, Lisa, Howard, Steve Peluso, and Mr. Drizzle, and suddenly the twins were surrounded. For twenty-one hours they had been voices on the radio, relying on one another for survival. Now, as their pulses returned to normal, there was jubilation and exhaustion.

But all of them were thinking some variation of the same thing: *When do we get to do that again?*

When Tommy Leibovitz joined the gathering, the twins had lots of questions. It turned out Barry was fine, but he would have to wait a couple of days for return transport. In the meantime his hosts were showing him the sights of Moscow. "He says that's okay with him," Tommy said. "He's always glad for an excuse to get out of school, and he's learning to like borscht."

Scott and Mark were about to drop from exhaustion by the time the crowd began to filter away. Major I would be leaving with Senator Glenn. As space-travel veterans, they had a lot to talk over, and the senator's office would arrange with the Russian government for Major I's trip home. Also going with them in the back of the limousine was a pet carrier full of rodents.

Richard Nixon, on the other hand, was unnecessary, the cosmonaut said. "Every time I attempted to take his blood in a tube the way I was supposed to do, he managed to elude from my hands. For that reason, the canine experiment has been a failure."

"So what will happen to him now?" Mark wanted to know.

Major Ilyushin shrugged. "If he is lucky, perhaps he can live in a cage in a laboratory and undergo new experiments until he dies of being an old dog."

"That's if he's *lucky*?" Mark said.

"Mom and Dad—" Scott began, but Mom and Dad were already shaking their heads.

"Major Nelson is enough dog, just like you two are enough kids," Dad said.

Grandpa stepped in. "Actually," he said, "I'd been thinking about getting a mutt of my own. If the Russian people don't mind, that is."

Senator Glenn climbed into the backseat of his

limousine and rolled down the window. The *Crazy 9* crew waved.

"It was really fantastic to meet you," said Mark.

"We'll never forget it," said Scott, "and all you've done for us. But could I ask for one more thing?"

"Sure, what's that?" the senator said.

"Could we have your autograph?"

Senator Glenn smiled. "I don't mind, but turnabout's fair play. What if after that, you give me yours?"

Over the next couple of days, Senator Glenn squared things with NASA. Even though he was, as he said, just a washed-up old astronaut, there were still some folks at the space agency who listened to him. It was also Senator Glenn who had intervened to keep Steve Peluso out of trouble with his father. From now on, it looked like anytime Steve wanted to work on a space project with that O'Malley girl and those Kelly twins, it would be okay with him.

Of course, the boys did not escape without a lecture—this one delivered by Mrs. O'Malley at dinner at Grandpa's house that night.

"What you did was brave, and it turned out well this time," she said, "but you took a huge risk, and at many points along the way things might have gone cata-strophically wrong. It takes experience to do a good job assessing which risks are worth taking. You'll understand that when you're older. For now, I hope you're done with space travel for a while."

Scott nodded. "I'm going to remember that," he said, and he meant it too. He was going to put it in his brain file under Reasons I'm Glad I'm Not Older . . . Yet.

Mark, who knew nothing of Scott's mental filing cabinet, turned on his brother: "Kiss-up."

"Am not," said Scott.

"Are too," said Mark.

Mr. and Mrs. Kelly looked at each other and sighed. "Boys?" said Mrs. Kelly.

"Yes, Mom?" said both twins at once.

"Your dad and I are really, really glad to have you back."

Author's Note

Astrotwins: Project Rescue is a crazy, made-up story about twelve-year-old twins in New Jersey who, with a lot of help from their friends and a little help from NASA, launch a space rescue in 1976.

The twins, Scott and Mark Kelly, are based on my brother and me, and there are additional real-life details about our family in the book too. We really did have a Grandpa Joe who lived near Greenwood Lake. Our parents were both police officers. We had a smart friend named Barry. My sixth-grade teacher was Mr. Hackess.

And yes, we acted like knuckleheads a lot of the time.

While Scott and I both grew up to be NASA astronauts, in truth, neither of us achieved Earth orbit till we were well-educated, highly trained grown-ups with years of experience flying military jets behind us. I doubt that anyone—even twelve-year-olds as fearless as my brother and I—could learn to operate a piece of machinery as complicated as a spacecraft as fast as the twins do in the story.

We would have given it our best shot, though!

Besides the true-life details from our personal history, *Project Rescue* includes true-life details from world history—like the 1976 presidential campaign, the Apollo-Soyuz missions, the difficulties faced by Vietnam veterans, and the diplomatic era known as détente.

The story also anticipates real-world events that came later, chiefly ongoing cooperation between what is now Russia and the United States in space. As I write, my brother, Scott, is about 249 miles above the Earth orbiting aboard the International Space Station (ISS) with two Russian cosmonauts, Gennady Padalka and Mikhail Kornienko. Like the fictional Captain Ilya Ilyushin, Scott blasted off in a Soyuz spacecraft from the Baikonur Cosmodrome.

Another real-world event presaged in the book is the experiment on the biological effects of living in space. One element of Captain Ilyushin's mission was to compare the health of two guinea pig littermates, one on Earth and one in orbit. Today, it's my brother and I who are the guinea pigs. During Scott's ISS year, scientists are running tests on each of us in hopes that comparing the results will help pave the way for future long-duration space missions, including a trip to Mars.

Finally, while *Project Rescue* may be far-fetched, the scientific and engineering basis for Scott's and Mark's flight is very much for real. I hope the following glossary will help you better understand some of the concepts— historical, scientific, and mathematical—that are referred to in the story.

Mark Kelly

Fall 2015

Glossary

AMU/Astronaut maneuvering unit: (Page 125) A backpack accessorized with hydrogen peroxide jets to enable space-walking astronauts to move around untethered, in other words, without a line linking them to the spaceship. In the story, someone flies to the rescue using an AMU, but in fact no astronaut ever did get to use one in space.

While the AMU was built and scheduled for service on two Gemini missions in 1966, it was not deployed. As of this writing, human beings have only performed four untethered spacewalks, three in 1984 using the Manned Maneuvering Unit, more advanced but similar to the AMU, and one in 1994 in a test of rescue equipment.

Apollo CSM: (Page 131) The Apollo space program, which flew from 1961–1972, put human beings on the moon. The CSM is the Command Service Module—a cone-shaped command component for the three-person crew and the equipment required for reentry and splashdown, and a cylindrical service component to provide propulsion, electrical power, and storage.

BASIC programming language: (Page 39) A programming language is language that communicates with a computer. Two professors developed BASIC (Beginner's All-purpose Symbolic Instruction Code) in 1964 with the idea that a consistent, easy-to-understand way to talk to computers would enable lots of people to use them.

And what do you know, it worked! In the 1970s and 1980s all sorts of people, including students like Howard Chin in the story, began fooling around with their own computers, most of them using BASIC to write programs. Updated versions of BASIC are still in use today.

cosmonauts: (Page 11) The space program of the U.S.S.R., later Russia, calls its astronauts cosmonauts. Of course, from their point of view, the U.S. calls its cosmonauts astronauts.

détente: (Page 70) The French word literally means easing of tension. It was used by the United States and Russia in the 1970s to indicate deliberate improvement in relations for the sake of promoting world peace.

Drizzle fuel: (Page 54) In *Astrotwins: Project Blastoff*, Jenny's science teacher, Mr. Drizzle, has formulated a uniquely powerful rocket fuel based on a chemical compounds similar to sugar. It is put to use again in this story.

Sugar propellants do exist, but none is anywhere nearly as powerful as the fictional Drizzle fuel.

EVA/Extra-vehicular activity: (Page 125) NASA devised the term extravehicular activity or EVA in the early 1960s to describe astronauts leaving a spacecraft, either to "walk" in space or to walk on the moon. The first person to perform an EVA was Russian cosmonaut Alexey Leonov in 1965, and it lasted twelve minutes.

g-forces: (Page 130) A measurement of acceleration used to describe gravitational effect. A force of 1-G means acceleration is the same as that caused by Earth's gravity. Astronauts in a spacecraft accelerating at greater than 1-G are pressed against their seats and feel heavier than normal.

gyroscope: (Page 143) A gyroscope is a device made up of an axle that is free to move any which way, and a wheel that spins around it. Angular momentum keeps the spinning wheel mostly stable, enabling the device to measure how the axle is placed in space at any given moment, in other words its orientation. A gyroscope is the basis of the system that keeps a spacecraft or a boat stable.

ICBM/intercontinental ballistic missile: (Page 50) A guided rocket aimed at a target at least 3,400 miles away. ICBMs are often designed to carry nuclear warheads.

Many of today's are still based on the work of World War II German scientists, including Wernher von Braun who moved to the United States after the war. In the United States and the Soviet Union, early ICBMs were the basis of many space launch systems, including the Russian R-7, and the American Atlas, Redstone, Titan and Proton.

Today, a much updated R-7 is still used to launch the Russian Soyuz, marking more than fifty years of operational history of engineer Sergei Korolyov's original design. In the story, the English-speaker who helps Barry out at Star City is based on Korolyov's widow.

microfilm: (Page 12) A length of film containing tiny (micro) photographs of documents. Before computers became common as storage devices, libraries used to save old newspapers and magazines on microfilm because it was durable and took up little space. If, like the Kelly twins in the story, a patron wanted to refer to an old issue of *TIME* magazine, he or she found the appropriate spool of microfilm and ran it through a machine that projected the enlarged image so it could be read.

orbit: (Page 54) The path one body in space—such as a planet, satellite, spaceship, or comet, follows around a more massive body such as the sun. Until the early twentieth century when Albert Einstein's general theory of relativity explained that gravity is actually a result of the curvature of space-time, it was thought that orbital properties were dictated by Newtonian physics. Even now, orbital calculations made using Newton's laws are close enough to be practically useful.

parabola: (Page 147) An arc made up of points in a plane each one of which is the same distance from a given line (the directrix), and a given point not on the line (the focus). In ideal conditions, an object flung from Earth and brought back by gravity—such as a rocket or a baseball—follows a path in the shape of a parabola.

Pythagorean theorem: (Page 80) The description of the relationship between the three sides of a triangle that contains one 90-degree angle—a right triangle. It states that the square of the hypotenuse (the side opposite the 90-degree angle) is equal to the sum of the squares of the other two sides. It is named for Pythagoras, a Greek philosopher who lived 2,500 years ago. The Pythagorean theorem is helpful in geography, navigation, architecture and engineering, among many other things.

range rate: (Page 184) The distance (range) to something divided by the speed (rate) at which it is being approached. So if you are a spacecraft approaching a space station that is five miles away at a speed of five miles per minute, your range rate is one minute.

Salyut: (Page 12) From 1971–1986, the Soviet Union placed six space stations in Earth orbit, four for scientific purposes and two for military reconnaissance purposes. This was the Salyut program. Among its goals was research into the problems of long-term living in space.

In the story, Barry, Mark, and Scott read about the tragic deaths of the first three cosmonauts to live aboard Salyut 1. In the summer of 1976, when the story takes place, *Salyut 4* was still in orbit. The fate of the fictional Major Ilyushin's Salyut is not the same as the actual fate of *Salyut 4*, which orbited until intentionally being brought back to Earth in 1977. Also, in reality, the Soviet Union sent only teams of three cosmonauts, not individuals, to live there.

sextant: (Page 83) A tool to measure the angle between any two objects, for example stars. The primary use of a sextant is to determine the angle between an object in space and the horizon to help with navigation. A traditional sextant is made up of a frame shaped like a piece of pie one-sixth of a circle in size, two mirrors and a telescope.

Skylab: (Page 14) The United States' first space station, Skylab was launched in 1973. Three crews of three astronauts visited it in orbit, each mission establishing a new record for human endurance in space. Skylab included a solar observatory, a workshop, closet-sized private sleeping areas for the astronauts, and even a shower. Hundreds of experiments were carried out, improving understanding of Earth's geography, the sun's corona, and the comet Kohoutek, among many other things.

NASA was ready in case the Skylab astronauts got into trouble. They had two astronauts standing by to launch a rescue in a modified Apollo CSM fitted with seats for five astronauts instead of the usual three. Happily, no rescue mission ever had to fly, and the last astronauts left Skylab in 1974.

NASA officials expected Skylab to remain in orbit until the early 1980s and even made plans to refurbish it. What they didn't count on was a glitch in the sunspot cycle yielding high radiation that caused orbit to deteriorate. The anticipated crash of the 77-ton space station created a worldwide sensation complete with Skylab-themed disco parties and souvenir hard hats even as NASA reassured earthlings that the odds of anyone being hurt were a mere one in one hundred fifty two.

As it happened, no one was hurt when Skylab re-entered the atmosphere on July 13, 1979. Most of it burned up or fell into the Indian Ocean as expected, but some debris did land in and around the small town of Balladonia, Australia. Today museums in the region commemorate the event.

Soyuz: (Page 84) The word, which means "union," refers both to the human space flight program begun by the

Soviet Union in the early 1960s, to the Soyuz spacecraft, and to the Soyuz rocket. As of this writing, everyone visiting the International Space Station has traveled there on a Soyuz spacecraft and will travel back home the same way.

In the story, Major Ilyushin is expecting to ride home from his Salyut space station on the Soyuz spacecraft that is docked outside. Like the Apollo CSM, the Soyuz spacecraft has room for a crew of three.

thrust: (Page 11) The verb means the same as push, so you can thrust something into the sky, like a rocket or a javelin. In aerospace, thrust is the measurement of how much force fuel provides when it combusts and expels gasses.

Thrust is often measured in units called newtons, named for Sir Isaac Newton, the English scientist who first described the laws of motion. One newton is the amount needed to accelerate a kilogram (which on Earth would weigh roughly 2.2 pounds) of mass at the rate of one meter (roughly 39 inches) per second squared. As Mark explains to his mom in the story, if you are trying to move something heavy up beyond the atmosphere, you need a lot of thrust.

Titan rocket: (Page 46) A family of seven American rockets built from 1959 until 2005, Titan rockets were designed to serve as ICBMs to launch weapons and for launching vehicles into space. NASA's ten Gemini missions of the mid-1960s were lifted into orbit atop Titan II rockets. The first Titan rockets were powered by liquid oxygen, which had to be stored at very low temperatures and was therefore impractical. Starting with Titan II, the rockets were powered by hypergolic fuel, meaning two chemicals that ignited when combined.

In the story, the Titan rocket is powered by the fictional Drizzle fuel, which delivers enough thrust to launch an Apollo CSM, bigger and heavier than the Gemini capsules. The real Apollo missions, which include the extra weight of lunar landers, were launched atop Saturn rockets. Today you can see a real Titan II rocket, six stories tall, at the Titan Missile Museum near Tucson, Arizona.

trigonometry: (Page 78) The word comes from the Greek and means measuring triangles. As Barry explains to Scott and Mark in the story, it is used in astronomy, geography, and navigation. It is also fundamental to the study of light and sound waves and so has applications in music, medicine, chemistry, seismology, meteorology and even videogame development.

The trigonometric functions sine, cosine, and tangent are the relationships between the angles of a right triangle (one with one 90-degree angle) and its signs. If you know the length of one side of the triangle and the measure of one angle (besides the right angle), you can calculate the length of the other two sides.

Sources

Cadbury, Deborah, *Spacerace: The Epic Battle between America and the Soviet Union for Dominion of Space.* New York: HarperCollins, 2006.

Carpenter, M. Scott, et. al. We Seven: *The Classic Story of the Heroes Who Launched America into Space.* New York: Simon & Schuster, 1962, 1990.

Cernan, Eugene with Don Davis. *The Last Man on the Moon.* New York: St. Martin's/Griffin, 1999.

Collins, Michael. *Carrying the Fire: An Astronaut's Journey.* New York: Farrar, Straus & Giroux, 1974, 2009.

Fishman, Charles. (2015 January/February) "5200 Days in Space." *The Atlantic Monthly*, Vol. 315, No. 1, pages 50–59.

Floca, Brian. *Moonshot, The Flight of Apollo 11.* New York: Simon & Schuster, 2009.

Kranz, Gene. *Failure is Not an Option: Mission Control from Mercury to Apollo 13 and Beyond.* New York: Simon & Schuster, 2000, 2009.

Mullane, R. Mike. *Do Your Ears Pop in Space?* New York: John Wiley & Sons, 1997

Mullane, R. Mike. *Riding Rockets: The Outrageous Tales of a Space Shuttle Astronaut.* New York: Scribner, 2006.

Pogue, William R. *How Do You Go to the Bathroom in Space?* New York: Tor, 1999.

Hitt, David, Owen Garriott and Joe Kerwin. *Homesteading Space, The Skylab Story.* Lincoln, Nebraska: University of Nebraska Press: 2008.

Excellent online resource
https://www.nasa.gov/audience/forstudents/index.html

Astrotwins: Project Rescue
By Mark Kelly
Reading Group Guide

About the Book

Mark and Scott Kelly, who are mostly known for getting in trouble, are finally back from their first space adventure. The twins have wanted to explore space ever since they were little and watched Neil Armstrong walk on the moon. And when they hear that a Russian cosmonaut is trapped inside the Salyut space station now orbiting 220 miles above the surface of the Earth, they wish they could find a way to help.

While staying in the countryside at their grandfather's house with their friend Jenny (a.k.a. Egg), the twins repurpose a NASA Titan 2 rocket ship being stored nearby. Complete with space suits and snacks, the twins take off to rescue the Russian spacecraft. Will they ever see their family or their grandfather's backyard again? Written by astronaut Mark Kelly, *Astrotwins— Project Rescue* brings the world of an astronaut to life in an exciting adventure tale.

Prereading Questions

1. What is the value of helping someone in need? Is there anything in it for you? How far would you go to help someone—even if it meant your life could be in danger?

2. What kind of skills might you need to plan a launch into space for a rescue mission?

Discussion Questions

1. What is the relationship between Mark and Scott? Give examples from the book as evidence of how they interact.

2. Mark didn't get to go on the first launch. Why would he have an advantage for being one of the astronauts this time?

3. Whom among the group of friends do you think should be the new astronauts?

4. What triggered Mark and Scott's interest in current events? Why did they want to continue to learn about events in the world?

5. Mark and Scott were angry they hadn't been told about the plans NASA had for Greenwood Lake. Why were they angry? How would you feel if you were left out of plans with a friend? Has that ever happened to you? How did you feel?

6. What advantages did the kids have when dividing up jobs for the new launch?

7. How does the time period in which the book takes place play a part in the story line? Support your answers with evidence from the book.

8. Is the setting an important part of the success of the mission? Explain why or why not.

9. Trace the changes evident in Mark and Scott as they plan and execute the rescue mission.

10. How did working together as a team benefit the launch? Would it have been possible if only two of them worked on it? What's the benefit of a team? In what instances is it better to work with others as a team than it is to work alone?

11. Discuss some of the information you learned in the novel about outer space and how to survive.

12. Explain why it was important to have the exact times and schedule figured for Mark and Scott's launch. What was the purpose of the multiple checklists the astronauts had to perform? Is there value in being organized? Explain your thoughts.

13. Talk about the strength and weaknesses of three of the main characters.

14. Why did the kids call their mission "Project Rescue"? Why was it important to rescue the Russian cosmonaut?

15. What consequences could happen in zero gravity? Why are those consequences important to consider? What are some of the problems for humans in zero gravity and how do the astronauts deal with it?

16. What part of the mission do you consider the most dangerous? Support your answer from evidence in the book.

17. Do you believe Mark and Scott will become astronauts when they grow up? If you don't think so, what job do you think they'd have instead?

18. Why were the twins worried about Barry being in the USSR? Discuss the political situation and the dangers he might face while in the Soviet Union.

19. What were some of the concerns of the twins as they approached the Salyut?

20. How did Scott feel about his brother's walk in space? What did he say and what did he promise? What was Mark's response?

21. Review the Author's Note in the back matter. Discuss the parts of the book that are real and the parts that are definitely fiction. How do you think Mark Kelly's life influenced this story? Explain your answers.

22. Compare the theme, setting, and plot of Kelly's story *Project Blastoff* with *Project Rescue*.

23. Describe how this story might be different if it had been told from another character's point of view? What other character could you visualize telling the story?

24. Review Chapter 13. How does it contribute to the plot's development?

25. What was Mark Kelly's point of view in writing the book, and how does his expertise help make the book real?

Writing

1. Write a descriptive passage about Mark and how he felt as the twins entered orbit and zero gravity. Include a conclusion.

2. Write a summary of the story and discuss the main idea and theme of the book.

3. Write a personal essay in the voice of one of the characters describing how they felt about the cosmonaut being stranded with no hope of rescue.

4. Write a letter to your senator asking for the US and NASA to intervene and rescue the cosmonaut.

5. Write a passage as if you were an astronaut. Describe a liftoff and what space looks like from the view in a spacecraft.

6. Write to explain how you personally feel about the space program and the role of astronauts.

Setting
1. Find examples from the book that show the events taking place during that time period.

2. Compare and contrast Grandpa Joe's home and location to that of the Kellys' home and explore how the setting helped the group of friends launch the twins into space.

3. Describe outer space based on the information the twins see on their flight.

4. Compare and contrast Mark and Scott's spacecraft with that of the Russian cosmonaut.

5. Read a nonfiction book about space and space travel, such as *Moonshot* by Brian Floca. Compare and contrast the two accounts of space.

Characters
1. Describe the personalities of Scott and Mark. Use examples from the book to support your description.

2. What kind of person is Jenny (or Egg)? Find three scenes from the book that show her personality and explain what she's like.

3. How did Mark develop his dislike of communists and what influence did it have on him? Explain.

4. What role did Tommy play in the rescue of the cosmonaut? Why was he important to the mission?

5. Compare and contrast two of the characters from the book. What qualities did they have that made them able to work together on the rescue project?

6. Choose an event that changed or affected one of the characters. Explain how it made a difference.

7. Which character in the book would likely be your friend? Explain your choice.

Plot

1. Identify five main points in the story's plot. Discuss why you chose those five and how they moved the story forward.

2. What is the main conflict in the story?

3. In what kind of order is the story presented? How does this order contribute to understanding the story?

4. Do you think it was unfair of NASA not to try to rescue the cosmonaut? How did this make the story move along? Have you had something unfair happen to you? How did you deal with it?

5. Read the NASA site about spacewalking: http://www.nasa.gov/audience/forstudents/k-4/stories/nasa-knows/what-is-a-spacewalk-k4.html. Compare and contrast Mark's spacewalk with NASA's explanation.

6. Identify the theme of the book, and explain how different parts of the plot contributed to the overall theme.

7. In what way did the help of John Glenn add to the plot and success of the mission?

8. Did the ending of the book provide a satisfactory resolution? Why or why not?

Point of View and Structure

1. How was the story structured? How did that particular structure work to develop the story?

2. What point of view was used in the story? Choose one scene and rewrite it in first person.

3. What evidence in the first chapter led you to think a major plot point would occur later in the story? Provide examples to support your answer.

Vocabulary

1. Find a vocabulary word you are not familiar with. Using context clues, write a definition. Then look up the word in the glossary of the book or a science dictionary. Explain how close you came to defining the word correctly.

2. Use the glossary in the back of the book to select three to five words. Look up the words and learn more about the object or principle and the science behind them. Write to explain the selected words and give an example of how it applies or is used in the book.

3. Find two examples of figurative language and explain their meaning.

4. Locate two to three words in the book that you don't know. Rewrite the sentences containing the chosen words with their appropriate page numbers. Look up the chosen words in the dictionary and explain their meaning. Did it

help you understand the meaning? Write your own original sentences using your chosen words.

Science

1. Read a description of an actual astronaut's spacewalk. Compare and contrast the real spacewalk with Mark's spacewalk. Use the following link from NASA's website as reference:

https://www.nasa.gov/multimedia/imagegallery/image_feature_1098.html

2. Describe Newton's Three Laws of Motion. How did they apply in the story, and which ones were used?

3. What equipment helped keep the astronauts safe during the flight and spacewalk? Describe them and tell how each piece contributes to the overall safety of the astronauts.

4. Discuss the effects of zero gravity on the body as described in the story.

5. Why is it necessary to use stages of a rocket that drop away, and how does that work?

6. Explain the problem Russian cosmonaut Ilya Ilyushin faced and the consequences if he wasn't rescued.

Technology

1. What technology tools were used to prepare and carry out the launch and mission?

2. How did Barry communicate with Mission Control and the spacecraft? Explain the procedure and what it was called.

3. Discuss the design and parts of the suit Mark wore on the space walk and how it addressed his needs.

4. In the novel, Mark states that the Russians are going to patch Howard through to their Mission Control Center. Look up the definition here: http://www.macmillandictionary.com/us/dictionary/american/patch-through. Explain why Howard had to be patched through.

5. Identify and summarize the different technologies the kids used to send the twins into space.

Engineering

1. Engineering is based on repeating and testing the process until the best design possible emerges. What flaw did the group have in their engineering of the spacecraft? Is it possible to succeed in an engineering mission on the first attempt? How is this different from the usual engineering process?

2. What did the group have to do to launch the rocket, and why?

3. What parts and activities contributed to the mission's success? Give examples.

4. How did the kids address specific issues relating to the mission? How was engineering important to their problems and solutions?

Mathematics

1. Give a definition of *trigonometry*. Explain how this branch of mathematics helped during the space mission rescue.

2. Explain *sine*, *cosine*, and *tangent* as they relate to trigonometry.

3. In the novel, Barry explains the Pythagorean theorem to Scott and Mark. Use your own words to explain the theorem and the different mathematical words in it.

4. Find the definition of square roots here or on a similar site. http://www.math.com/school/subject1/lessons/S1U1L9DP.html. Compare the definition to Barry's explanation in the novel. List some examples of square roots.

5. How is space navigation determined using stars as explained in the book? In your own words, explain the relationship between navigation and trigonometry.

6. Describe and define an angle. Look up right angles, obtuse angles, and acute angles and draw an example of each.

Extension Activities

1. Draw a model of Mission Control and label the different parts using the description from the book.

2. Create a timeline of the days and events leading up to the launch and the mission to rescue the cosmonaut.

3. Research Pythagoras and the time in which he lived. Describe your findings and his contribution by making a presentation.

4. Give your opinion about space and space flight in an essay. Support your arguments.

5. Identify three examples about history from the book's setting. What events can you find that show historical

information? Discuss by writing about those events in relation to the twins' world.

6. Write a poem that reflects the feelings and emotions expressed by either Scott or Mark as they travel through space.

7. Write a three-act play based on three important scenes from the book. Break into groups and present the play to your classmates.

8. In your library, look at all the books classified in the Engineering section. Choose three-to-five books and browse them. Read one of them and locate anything in the book that relates to *Project Rescue*. Describe those actions or events that are similar.

9. Look up John Glenn and his contributions to space. Make a list of questions you might ask if you were to interview him.

10. Read about microgravity at http://www.nasa.gov/centers/glenn/shuttlestation/station/microgex.html. Then explain microgravity in your own words, and discuss how it was portrayed in the novel.

11. Read about G-forces here: https://www.faa.gov/pilots/safety/pilotsafetybrochures/media/Acceleration.pdf. What level of G-forces or G-loads did Mark and Scott experience and under what circumstances? Summarize your explanation and the times when the twins experienced the forces.

12. Read about John Glenn's Friendship 7 flight here: http://www.nasa.gov/content/astronaut-john-h-glenn-

jr-with-mercury-friendship-7-spacecraft. Make a chart to show his velocity, apogee, and time in space. On the chart, compare his numbers to the statistics of the twins' flight during their rescue mission.

13. The spacecraft used solar panels for energy. Explore solar energy by reading about it here:

http://www.alliantenergykids.com/energyandtheenvironment/renewableenergy/022400

Then build a simple solar oven like this one:

http://www.alliantenergykids.com/wcm/groups/wcm_internet/@int/@aekids/documents/document/mdaw/mdiy/~edisp/022819.pdf. Practice safety and do the activity with adult supervision.

14. Explore how a sextant works by reading about navigating with one: http://www.pbs.org/wgbh/nova/shackleton/navigate/escapeworks.html

15. Write interview questions for Mark and Scott. Then also write the answers that you think Mark and Scott might give.

16. Reenact the first meeting between Mark and Major Ilyushin. Then present this scene as a skit to the class.

17. Write an explanation about why the Russian spaceship exploded.

18. Draw and label three triangles. Make one have a right angle, one have an acute angle, and the third have an obtuse angle.

19. Read the author's note. Then watch a video of Mark and

Scott Kelly's mission for the International Space Station: https://www.youtube.com/watch?v=Bo2igadkAHU. Discuss the value of a study like this relating to space flight.

Guide written by Shirley Duke, a children's freelance writer.

Did you LOVE reading this book?

Visit the Whyville...

IN THE MIDDLE BOOK HIVE

Where you can:

- Discover great books!
- Meet new friends!
- Read exclusive sneak peeks and more!

Log on to visit now!
bookhive.whyville.net

CAMP + COOKIES = FRIENDS FOREVER

"Hand this to the BFFs who aren't quite ready for Brashares's *The Sisterhood of the Traveling Pants*."
—*Bulletin of the Center for Children's Books*

FOUR VERY DIFFERENT GIRLS BECOME BEST FRIENDS WHILE AT MOONLIGHT RANCH SUMMER CAMP. WHEN LIFE ISN'T PICTURE-PERFECT, THERE ARE TWO THINGS THESE CAMPERS CAN COUNT ON: FRIENDSHIP AND COOKIES.

BULLYING.
BE A LEADER
AND STOP IT.

Do your part to stop bullies in their tracks.

Protect yourself and your friends with STOPit. It's easy.
It's anonymous. It's the right thing to do.

"Never let a bully win." - Derek Jeter

Download the app today!

TURN 2
FOUNDATION, INC.

 STOPiT.